PUFFIN PLUS

Sports shots and still-life, family groups and bouncing babies – they're all within range of your camera if you know how to use it properly. And this book tells you how. It will help you improve your photographs and get the most from your equipment, whether you have an Instamatic or the most sophisticated 35 mm camera on the market.

Professional photographer Christopher Wright explains all the photographic processes simply and clearly. You can confine yourself to learning how to take good photographs or you can learn about the technical side too. Once you've improved your basic skills, you can learn how to develop your own films, print your own pictures and make enlargements.

First published very successfully in 1979 as *The Puffin Book of Photography*, this comprehensive handbook will prove an invaluable aid for any would-be camera buff.

CHRISTOPHER WRIGHT

SNAP!

A HANDBOOK OF PHOTOGRAPHY
FOR BEGINNERS

ILLUSTRATED BY GRAHAM ROUND
PHOTOGRAPHS BY CHRISTOPHER WRIGHT

PUFFIN BOOKS

Puffin Books, Penguin Books Ltd, Harmondsworth, Middlesex, England
Penguin Books, 625 Madison Avenue, New York, New York 10022, U.S.A.
Penguin Books Australia Ltd, Ringwood, Victoria, Australia
Penguin Books Canada Ltd, 2801 John Street, Markham, Ontario, Canada L3R 1B4
Penguin Books (N.Z.) Ltd, 182–190 Wairau Road, Auckland 10, New Zealand

First published as *The Puffin Book of Photography* 1979
Reissued under the present title 1981

Text and photographs copyright © Christopher Wright, 1979
Illustrations copyright © Graham Round, 1979
All rights reserved

Made and printed in Great Britain by
Butler & Tanner Ltd, Frome and London
Set in Monophoto Times

Except in the United States of America, this book is sold subject
to the condition that it shall not, by way of trade or otherwise, be lent,
re-sold, hired out, or otherwise circulated without the
publisher's prior consent in any form of binding or cover other than
that in which it is published and without a similar condition
including this condition being imposed on the subsequent purchaser

Contents

A note about the photographs 7
1 Getting started 11
2 Printing in daylight 24
3 What are 'settings'? 34
4 Focusing and people 46
5 All sorts of cameras 65
6 Dark-room printing 81
7 Closer and closer 95
8 Photography indoors 112
9 Processing your own films 124
10 Making enlargements 136
11 And also... 156
12 Putting it right 170
 Index 181

A note about the photographs

Many of the photographs in this book are quite ordinary. To take them, I used a range of different cameras. Many of these were simple and inexpensive. It will not be long before you are able to take photos that are just as good, and perhaps a lot better.

To make the photographs more interesting, I have made a note each time showing the camera I used. Here are some drawings of the types of cameras used. Sometimes I have used the 'best' camera for the subject, and sometimes I have used the least likely. In nearly every case I could have used any of the seven basic types listed below. In this list I have given a brief description of the particular model which *I* used for this book.

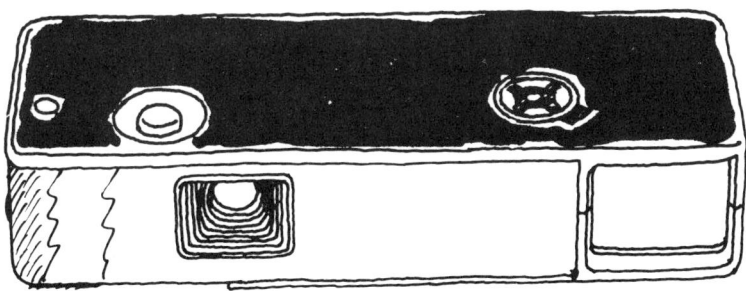

110
Cartridge

5 weather symbols to set.
No focusing.
Built-in flash-cube holder

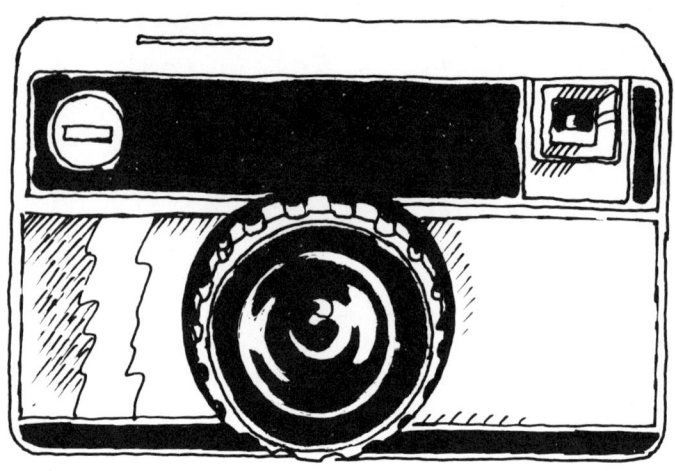

126
Cartridge

No weather symbols.
No focusing.
Built-in flash-cube holder

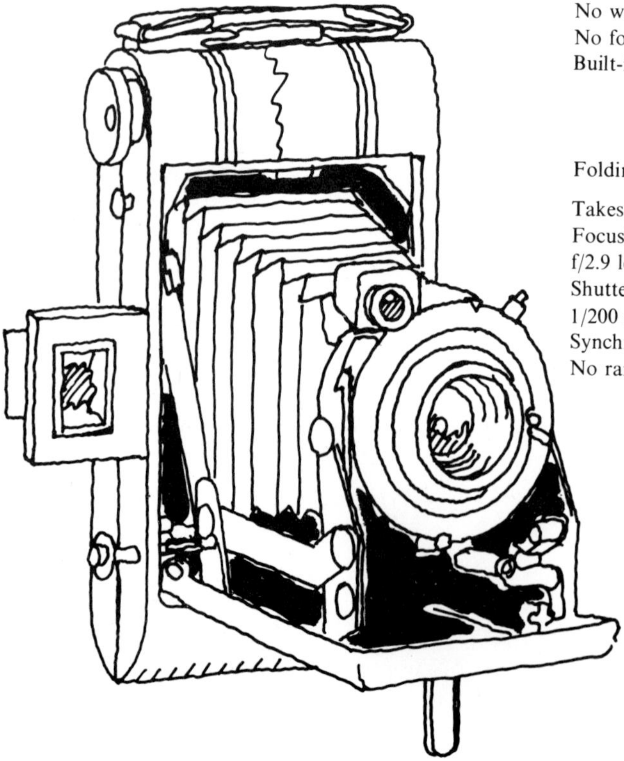

Folding

Takes 12 on 120 film.
Focusing down to 1 metre.
f/2.9 lens.
Shutter speeds 1/25 to
1/200 second and 'B'.
Synchronized for flash.
No rangefinder

35 mm

Focusing down to 1 metre.
f/2.8 lens.
Shutter speeds 1/30 to
1/250 second and 'B'.
Synchronized for flash.
No light meter.
No rangefinder.
Bright-line viewfinder

Twin-lens reflex

Takes 12 on 120 film.
f/3.5 lens.
Focusing down to 1 metre.
Shutter speeds 1 second to
1/500 and 'B'.
Synchronized for flash.
No light meter.
Quite an old model

Single-lens reflex

Takes 35 mm film.
Focusing down to 250 mm.
Shutter speeds 1 second to 1/1000 and 'B'.
Synchronized for flash.
'Through-the-lens' light meter

Box

Takes 8 on 620 film.
No exposure setting.
Focusing lever for close-ups.
'B' setting on shutter.
No flash facility

1 Getting started

Do you have a camera of your own? It doesn't matter if not, because I'm sure you'll be able to borrow one for a couple of days. For this first chapter, any type of camera will do. Even an old one. There's no need to borrow a model costing several hundred pounds! You are going out on a range of interesting assignments.

Imagine you are on an adventure trail in a place you've never visited before. In this way everything you see will be worth photographing. The only camera you have with you will be the one in your pack – and that is the camera you already own, or have managed to borrow.

Let's say that this camera will only take eight pictures and is loaded with a black-and-white film. When doing all your own photography at home, you will find black-and-white film much easier to use and process than colour film. Now, what are you going to photograph in these 'strange' surroundings? Houses? A view of the local scenery could be very interesting. Then some people. An animal? Perhaps some toys or models. Flowers or insects. What about the insides of the buildings?

Surely your camera will not do all of this! Are you sure? Have you tried? That is what this book is all about. Go out and take some pictures; look at the results, and then read how to do it properly! Cheap cameras if they are used carefully can take excellent pictures of the most unlikely subjects. Look through the photographs in this book and you will see what you can do with some of the cheapest, as well as some of the most expensive cameras.

> *Most important!*
>
> If you are thinking of buying a camera, don't do so until you have read this book. You may change your mind about the type that would be best for you. By 'best' I mean the one that you would find easy to use, would perform well on the type of subject that interests you; and perhaps, most important of all, is the one you can best afford.

Now to work. Imagine you have only twenty-four hours before your adventure trail is over. There are only eight exposures on your film. (If your camera has more exposures, then take several photographs of anything that specially interests you.) You may have to buy a roll of black-and-white film. If you have no idea how the camera is loaded then take it with you when you buy the film and ask the person in the shop to load it for you. Some shops may have **outdated** black-and-white film which will work perfectly well. You should only be charged half price for

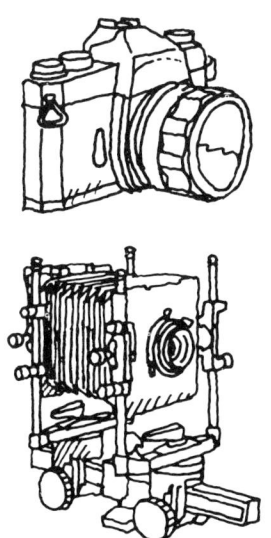
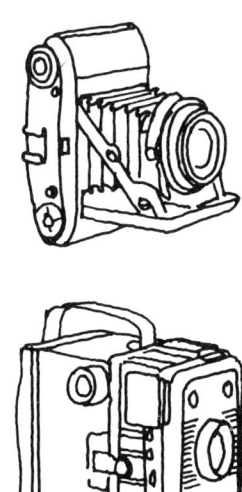

this film. Watch how the camera is loaded and try and remember for the next time. Most photographic shops get asked to load films, so they will not think your request strange.

As well as there being different manufacturers' makes of film, there are several different types. The make of film is not as important as the type. General purpose films are called **medium speed**. They are exactly what they say. General Purpose. Use them when the weather is bright. In the winter (or on dull days) **high speed** films are better. If in doubt, get a High Speed film. You can use it even on sunny days without any serious problems.

An exposure guide should be packed with the film. If your camera has **settings** on the front then you will need one of these guides. Some simple cameras have a sunny/cloudy setting, or perhaps nothing at all. Other cameras will have **shutter speeds** and **apertures** which need setting before taking a photograph. An exposure guide tells you how to set these shutter speeds and apertures according to the weather conditions. A sunny day is obviously brighter than a cloudy day. Settings allow you to control the amount of light reaching the film. Most cameras with **settings** can be used even on the dullest days.

As we go through each of our 'assignments' I shall only be giving some basic help. Don't be worried about not knowing what to do. Making mistakes is one of the best ways to learn. Perhaps none of these first eight photographs will be very good. In later chapters I shall explain in much greater detail what to do. Some cameras will obviously be better than others for tackling different jobs, but even the most elementary camera will take on almost any job once you know how. When you have finished reading this book and have carried out the assignments, *you will know how*. But to be a photographer you have to take photographs. Wait no longer. Get started now!

Photo No. 1 – a house

I don't think anyone will argue with me when I say that all ordinary cameras will be suitable for photographing views and houses. I can't see a professional photographer using a snap-shot camera, but then he would have several cameras to choose from. At the moment you probably have no choice. Take this book with you (and your loaded camera) and go out of doors. Look up at your house. Too close? Then go down the road a bit. Look in the viewfinder. You know what your house looks like, and are probably so familiar with it that it doesn't seem to make a very interesting picture.

That is why I have asked you to imagine that this picture is to take back as a record of your adventure trail. In any case, you want the result to be as good as possible. Some of the road or surrounding houses would be worth including to show your house in its setting. Of course, you don't have to photograph your own house. Any house will do.

It is very important not to tilt the camera to get the roof in the picture. You will see why later. You must go back further and hold the camera level. Try and get something interesting in the picture close to the camera. You might have to ask a neighbour if you can go in their garden to look out from between some trees or bushes. These will make a frame for your house.

Folding

What about the exposure settings? If it is a *very* dull day, a simple camera will not work unless you have loaded it with a high speed film. Where possible, use exposure settings from the exposure guide that comes with the film. Remember to set the focusing mark on your lens to the far distance (**infinity**) if it is adjustable, and hold the camera still. Breathe in. Hold your breath. Press the shutter release slowly and steadily. Slowly, slowly, slowly – click. The picture has been taken and the camera held steady. Don't stab at the release or you will shake the camera.

No click? Then you may not have set the shutter. Some camera shutters will set themselves, but others have a lever that has to be pulled across to wind the shutter mechanism up. *Now wind the film on.* You don't want to take more than one picture on frame number one! With some cameras you have to wind the film on before the camera will work again. Others have nothing to prevent you from taking more than one exposure on the same piece of film.

Photo No. 2 – a view

You now have to find a suitable view. It's not worth going very far at this stage. The real purpose of this exercise is to get some negatives which you can print and examine. There is an easy way of making your own prints without any sort of dark-room, and we'll come to that in Chapter 2. A quick walk down the road and around the block should help you see something worth recording. There is no need to climb a mountain! Again, you are so familiar with your surroundings that you probably never notice them and that is why I want you to imagine you are seeing them for the first time. I suppose even the local rubbish dump would look interesting to someone!

Photo No. 3 – people

As well as the exposure, there is a further setting you may have to make on your camera: focusing. **Focusing** means making a chosen part of the photograph sharp (clear). You do this by altering the distance the lens is from the film. There may be a lever to pull, the front of the lens to turn, or the whole front of the camera to pull out. Some cameras will have no focus settings. A box camera will be in focus from infinity (far distance) to as close as two or three metres. Instamatic (cartridge loading) type cameras without focus settings will be in focus as close as one or one and a half metres. You should now ask a friend – someone with great patience would be an advantage – to come with you.

You are going to attempt an outdoor photograph of a friend. There is no need to come very close. A full-length figure can look very good. Watch the background and don't ask the person to stand to attention. If your friend can be doing something (such as working on a bicycle or reading) they will feel at ease. You can either call, and take the picture as soon as your friend looks up, or just take it without warning. There is no *need* for the person to be looking at the camera, but don't worry about this. Try to get a *natural* looking photo.

35 mm

If you take your camera with you to the shops, you can get pictures of people when they do not know there is a camera about. You have to work with the camera at your waist and pointing in the right direction. If you start peering into the viewfinder and altering the settings you will give yourself away and your subjects will go off hastily and give you some funny looks! The photograph below was taken in this way, through the back of a park seat. The children had no idea they were being photographed and so they look completely natural. Photographing people at work or play is much more satisfactory than posing them.

T.L.R.

Photo No. 4 – people running

I hope your friend kept still. If he or she moved suddenly you will find that the image is blurred. You *can* take pictures of people moving but you have to swing the camera round to follow them. I'll be explaining how to do it in Chapter 6. For the moment, have a try. Get your friend to run sideways past you (about three metres away from the camera) and as the camera swings to follow him, press the shutter. Don't worry if you don't think it will work. The result will teach you a lot.

Photo No. 5 – animals

Now find an animal and take a photograph of it in its natural setting. A cat on a length of window sill if your camera won't focus close enough for the cat on its own. Later on there will be chances for greater things.

126
Cartridge

Get into a position with the camera held down low and use the sky to get a plain background for a picture like this

Photo No. 6 – toys and models

I'm sure you've seen films of prehistoric monsters where much of the photography has been done with models. Space films are done in the same way. If you choose realistic backgrounds then most people will be fooled. If you were to put a model train on the pavement, it would only look like a model. Put it emerging from a tunnel and it will look much more real.

Photographing a toy or model is your next job. The smaller the object, the closer you will need to come. Some cameras will definitely be better than others. Some of you will know how to use a camera close up, but many of you will be inclined to give up at this stage. 'Impossible with my camera,' you will say. At the moment you may not know how to do it, but by the end of the book you will have discovered that most things are possible. I'm not going to tell you how to do it in this chapter. I want you to try, and if you make mistakes you must not worry.

Photo No. 7 – very close

Of course, you may have a camera that has no focus settings. I have already mentioned that you can come as close as one or two metres, and still keep your subject in sharp focus. But you are unlikely to be able to photograph small models from as far away as that. Even from one metre they will look too small to be seen properly. All right, suppose you get *really* close? Try this. Put a coin against a wall in the garden and look through the viewfinder from about two metres away. Then come closer and closer until the coin fills most of the viewfinder. Instead of a coin you could find an insect, flower, or anything small, but *do* go very close for this photograph.

Those of you who know what to do will probably make a good job of it. Others will find that although their cameras are able to focus very close, they will not do so well. There's a snag to close-up work even with cameras that focus close to the subject, unless

S.L.R.

you have a viewfinder that looks out *through* the lens. I shan't tell you the snag now. Just take the photograph and wait for the results.

What about the simple non-focusing camera? Don't give up at this stage. Go as close as you like and press the shutter. The result will be no good at all I'm afraid, but at least you will discover what happens. In Chapter 8 I will tell you how you can photograph insects with a simple non-focusing camera and get good results. You may think that you are wasting your time (and film), but I want you to become fully aware of your camera's good and bad points, and this way you will be able to overcome them.

Photo No. 8 – *indoors*

Now take your camera indoors. Persuade your friend to be photographed again and try to get a photograph by using either the light coming through the window, or the electric light if it is dark. Don't use flash or stand too close to a sunny window. That would be cheating!

There are two types of camera with which this is going to be very difficult. The cartridge loading camera with only a sunny/cloudy setting will have to be used close to a bright window or else you must use a flash. Try whichever one you wish. Of course, if you want to see what happens if you just press the shutter in ordinary room lighting (and in a way I hope you will) then go ahead.

The other camera which is difficult to use is the box camera (or simple camera with no lens settings). Here, instead of just pressing the shutter, see if there is a lever to allow you to take **time** exposures. Move the lever to 'T' for 'time' or 'B' for 'bulb' and hold the camera firmly down on a table. With a 'B' setting, press down the shutter and slowly count five. Release the shutter and breathe again. With a 'T' setting, press the shutter release and let go. After five seconds press the release again, or move it back to where it started. Don't forget to put the lever back from the time or bulb setting before using the camera out of doors. Five seconds might be too much or too little with your camera but you should get *something* on the negative. If you have an exposure meter then you will have no problems.

And don't forget to wind the film on. It's so easy to get more than one picture on the same negative with some cameras!

You had to make sure your camera was kept very still for that exposure. If you want to take a time photograph inside a building you must make sure that everyone stands very still too, or have an empty room. Try taking a time exposure inside your school hall when it's full of people if you have any film left, and you will see what I mean.

Remember to set the focusing. Focus for the main part of the picture. If you note all the settings (including the time of the exposure) you will be able to repeat or improve the photograph if you decide to take more on a later film.

You should now have completed eight exposures. If you have taken eight exposures but the film number says '7', then you have forgotten to wind on at some stage and taken two on one! You may not know exactly when you did this, but you still have one more to take, so use it up on any subject of your choice. If you have a longer film with more than eight exposures then you might as well use it all because you are going to get the film processed. Why not go back over all the assignments again? Already you will have learnt by experience, and you haven't even seen your first results – yet!

2 Printing in daylight

Getting your film developed

Towards the end of the book I am going to show you how to process your black-and-white films at home. For the time being you can take them to your local photographic dealer or chemist and ask for **process only** or **develop only**, which is the same thing. That means you will get negatives back, but not prints. There is a quick and easy way to make your own prints at home, and you do not even need a dark-room. They won't be very good, but cheaper and more fun than getting someone else to do them for you. Then in Chapter 6 you will find all you need to know to make really good prints in a home dark-room. But for printing this first film you do not need a dark-room – or chemicals – if you are not very particular about the results. This chapter tells you how.

Money may be no obstacle to you, and you will want to order prints when you take your film for processing, in which case go straight ahead and ask for **enprints**. These are enlarged prints from the whole of the negative. Hence the name. They will be larger than your negative, but the exact size will vary according to the original negative shape. Square negatives will make enprints about 89 mm by 89 mm, and rectangular negatives will make enprints about 89 mm by 127 mm. Rectangular negatives make bigger enprints than square ones. When you do your processing and printing at home you will be able to make your prints any size you choose.

If you have to choose between developing your films or printing your negatives, choose printing. Printing is where you can save money and get the results you want from your negatives. Processing your own films may not save money, but there are several 'tricks of the trade' which you can copy to improve results. For the time being, though, be content to let someone else do the film processing for you, unless you already know how to do it. Developing your films to make negatives is a rather risky process, and though with practice you will gain confidence and soon think nothing of it, there are several things you could do wrong at first.

Looking at your negatives

You may get your negatives back the next day, or you may have to wait for a week. How will they look when you get them back? Let's assume that your camera was working properly. If it was, you are bound to get *something* on your film. Open the folder of negatives and tip them out gently on to a clean piece of paper. More than likely they are all together in a pile. Negatives must be handled by the edges. You will see that one side is shiny and the other dull. If you touch the shiny side by accident you can wipe the finger marks off with a soft handkerchief. Marks on the dull (**emulsion**) side are very difficult to remove. Rubbing them will only scratch the film. The dull side is the picture. The shiny side is the backing (or film) on which the emulsion containing the picture is coated.

If you look through a negative with the shiny side towards you, the picture will be the right way round. At least, the left hand side of the subject will be on the left, and the right hand side on the right. What will be the wrong way round are the tones. If the film is colour the colours will look very strange.

With all negatives, dark parts of your original scene will be pale and the bright parts will show dark. If you are only used to looking at colour transparencies where all the tones are correct, this may all look very strange to you. A negative is only half-way to the final print. The next stage puts all the tones back as they were, so the photograph then looks correct (prints from black-and-white negatives are still in black-and-white, of course).

Negative

Positive

If you need to hold your negatives against a *bright* light to see them properly, then they are **overexposed**, which means that they have received rather too much exposure to light when you were taking the picture. Don't worry. If you can see them by the bright light, you will still be able to get a print from them.

A properly exposed negative can be looked at with a sheet of white paper a few centimetres behind it, and show a full range of tones. This is a good standard to aim for, but for the moment you will be relieved to see anything at all on your film!

The other extreme to overexposure is **underexposure**. Not enough light reached the film when you pressed the shutter. The whole negative will look washed out and only pale tones will be there. Large areas of the negative may be completely clear. It will be very difficult to get a print from a negative like this, and I hope you do not have too many of them on your film!

Colour photography

It may be that you are only interested in taking *colour* photographs and are prepared to pay for the processing. Or perhaps you have seen a home-processing kit for colour that looks easy (and safe) enough to use. Work out the costs and the difficulties carefully. If you consider that black-and-white is still much cheaper, save the money towards a better camera. A few pounds saved on processing may buy quite a good second-hand camera. Later on – perhaps by the end of this book – you will feel more like taking on colour processing. I am recommending black-and-white at present because processing is relatively cheap, easy and safe. Above all, it is fun – because it works with the minimum of fuss and bother.

A way of taking colour pictures without having prints is to take colour slides. You can even make colour prints from colour slides easily at home, but work out the cost before making up your mind about this. The more I think about it, the more convinced I am that you will be well advised to start with black-and-white. You do not have to be so careful about exposure for one thing. Perhaps most important of all, when you are making your own black-and-white prints, you will be able to see what you are doing in your dark-room by using quite a bright safelight but more about that later. In any case, working with black-and-white film is a good introduction to using colour materials.

> There is a useful trick you can do with underexposed negatives which may be some consolation. Stand so that a light is coming from behind you. A window or table lamp will do. Hold the negative just by the corner, but with the dull (emulsion) side towards you. If you look at the negative with something black (or very dark) immediately behind it, the surface of the negative will appear as a positive print, with the dark tones light, etc. You may need to twist the negative about a bit before you see this happen. As I said, I suppose it is some consolation for an underexposed negative!
>
> What you are looking at is still really a negative. What makes it look like a positive is just a trick of the light.

Now to turn all your negatives into prints. This chapter only deals with a quick and easy way of making prints. If you already know how to make good prints by yourself, you can print your negatives straight away and pass on to the next chapter.

Printing paper

Photographic **printing paper** is sensitive to light and, before processing, has to be handled under dim lighting in a colour which will not affect the emulsion. When you have printed your negative on to this paper (you will discover how in a moment) there is no picture to be seen. The paper has to be **developed** in chemicals which will make the picture visible. However, if you leave out an untreated sheet of photographic paper in a bright light, the emulsion will eventually turn blue or pink. (The colour depends on the make of paper.) A long exposure to light turns the paper quite dark in colour, but a shorter exposure leaves it pale. The longer the exposure time, the darker the tone. Can you see the possibilities?

If you take a negative, flatten it against printing paper, and shine a bright light *through it*, you will find that this paper will not darken evenly. Where your negative is fairly clear, the paper will get darker. Where there are dark patches on your negative, the paper will stay nearly white. Your negative is making a positive print. (Fox Talbot, the famous pioneer of photography, made his first photographs in this way.) A main drawback with this system is that the paper goes on darkening after the negative has been removed. All the same, it will be a quick way of seeing your negatives as prints, and if you look at these prints in artificial light, they will not darken much further. Keep them in a drawer or between the pages of a book. Don't expect marvellous results because the paper never goes really dark and this limits the range of tones you can obtain. Now to make some prints.

What to buy

You will need photographic printing paper. If you ask your local photographic shop for **enlarging paper** (also called **bromide paper**) you will get the right sort. You can get a glossy surface, or a surface with a fine texture. There may be a choice of paper thickness. You may not have the opportunity to choose exactly the paper you want but neither the paper surface nor the paper thickness will affect your results very much. What is important is the **contrast grade**. I will deal with contrast grades in Chapter 4, but for now, I suggest you ask for a **normal** grade. Next choice would be a **contrasty** grade.

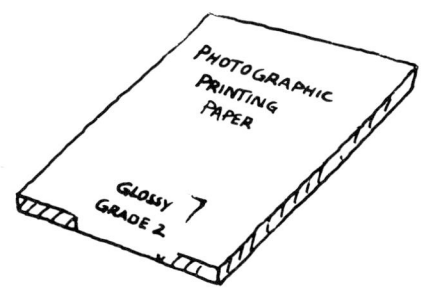

Treat this packet of paper with care. *Don't* open it up until you have read all of this chapter! If you are unable to get the right size for your negatives, then you can buy a larger size and cut it into pieces. Ask what sizes are available and see which size will cut the best without waste. There are likely to be packets of 25 or 100 sheets to choose from. This paper almost certainly won't be 'paper' at all, but a sort of plastic. This is easier to use than the older type of enlarging paper.

Making a print

You will also need a piece of glass at least as large as your negatives, but it can be quite a bit larger, and a piece of hardboard, chipboard or plywood the same size as the glass. If you have to get the glass cut to size, ask for the edges to be smoothed over so that it will be safe to handle. Some large spring paper clips (bulldog clips) or clothes pegs are the only other things you will need to make these prints.

You *must* open the packet of paper in complete darkness. Draw the curtains and if necessary hang a blanket over the window even when it is dark outside. The paper you are about to use will not change colour immediately in a partially darkened room, but the light *will* affect all the remaining sheets of paper and spoil them for later on when you want to use them with a photographic developer to make better prints. If you cannot make the room absolutely black, go into a cupboard or under the bedclothes at night with the curtains drawn. Later on you will find out how to see what you are doing by using a special light called a **safelight**.

Open your packet of paper and remove just a few sheets. Inside the outer envelope you may feel a black plastic inner envelope. Close both envelopes *before* turning on the room light. It will need a surprisingly bright light to affect the sheets of paper you have removed, so there is no need to hurry the next stage. Just keep them away from the window or a strong light bulb. Cut the paper to the correct size if necessary and put the spare pieces into a drawer or a book to protect them.

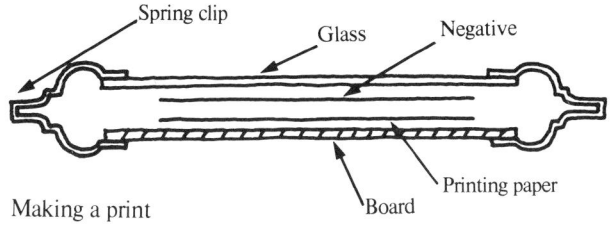

Making a print

Place the paper, with the emulsion side upwards, on top of your piece of board. The emulsion side will look either shiny or textured – possibly both. The paper side should be obvious and this is the side that rests on the board. Now place your negative with its dull (emulsion) side down on the emulsion side of the photographic paper. Then put your piece of glass over the two and finally clip the glass tightly to the board. Leave a margin of paper showing beyond the negative, and you will be able to check to see how much the paper has darkened during exposure.

Ready to go? Daylight – especially sunlight – will have the most rapid effect on the paper. Twenty or thirty seconds in bright sun will probably be sufficient exposure time for making a print. On a duller day maybe a few minutes will be needed. Indoors you can place the 'sandwich' close to a 100 watt light bulb, but check that it does not get too hot.

You will have some idea of how your print is getting on from the margin of paper showing round the negative. It may also help you to judge when your print is ready if you understand the difference between an overexposed and an underexposed negative. An overexposed negative is dense. Even when the paper margins have gone dark, not enough light will have penetrated the negative to have much effect on the picture. On the other hand, a thin (underexposed) negative will be fairly clear, and may need to be removed before the margins go dark. I expect that you will soon be able to estimate the exposure time.

Looking at the print

When you think the time is up, take your sandwich indoors and open it in a slightly darkened room. If most of the paper is too light, the time was too short. If everything has merged into a general darkness, then the exposure time was too long. If the print has some light – or even white – tones, *as well as* some dark areas, then your exposure time was probably correct. Remember, there will never be any *black* tones on prints made in this way, just pink or blue, depending on the *make* of paper.

There is nothing you can do to improve this particular print if it is too light. You would never be able to get it back under the negative to register exactly in the same position. Start again with a new piece of paper. Don't forget, if you need more paper, to open your packet *in the dark only*. You may be using the remainder of these sheets as dark-room printing paper later on, so no light must get to them yet.

> This type of printing is known as 'contact' printing as its name suggests. The negative is in contact with the paper. The alternative to contact print is enlarging, when the image from the negative is shone on to the paper by an enlarger. An enlarger is rather like a projector, but it usually shines downwards on to the paper.

Some of you may be fortunate enough to have a contact printing frame. This will make a sandwich of your negative and printing paper inside a wooden framework. The board at the back is hinged in the middle. It will be very difficult to get such a frame nowadays but years ago they were in common use. When you think the paper has had enough exposure, you bring the frame indoors and open one half of the back of the frame. The paper and negative cannot move out of register because the other half is still firmly trapped. If the paper is too pale, you close the frame and continue the exposure. If you *can* get a contact printing frame cheaply, I advise you to do so. When you make proper dark-room prints, which are described in Chapter 6, it will prove to be a very handy way of holding your paper and negative together.

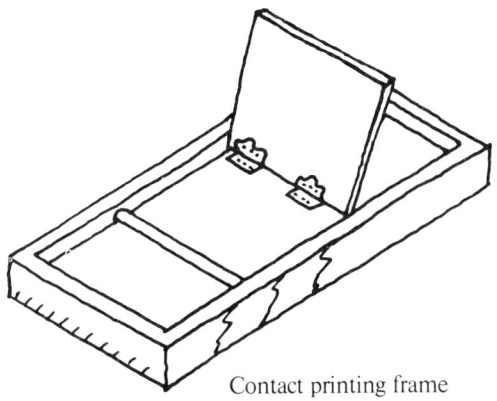
Contact printing frame

Some bromide (enlarging) paper will give very poor results. It will never get very dark. Don't blame the paper – it wasn't made to be used like this! But even wishy-washy results will enable you to see your negatives as positives. You can be sure that all photographic paper will give good results when you use photographic developer and a dark-room. Your dealer *may* know which make will be best for making prints in daylight. On the other hand, he may say that no make is suitable. Don't be put off. You are buying the packet so that you can make proper prints later on. At the moment you are just using a few sheets from it 'to have a go' at this type of daylight printing. You will be getting a taste of what is to come without having to make up a proper dark-room yet. But do be careful to open this packet *in the dark only*.

3 What are 'settings'?

You will have had a good look at the results of your first film by now. Out of doors, on a bright day, there is usually enough light to expose a negative sufficiently with any sort of camera. All types of camera should have been suitable for taking photographs of houses and views. Even a camera with no focusing adjustment will be focused correctly for distant objects.

Of course, you may not be able to find a sunny day for taking photographs. How can you adjust a camera to work satisfactorily on a dull day? If your camera has a range of **settings**, how do you choose the most suitable? It is probably best to answer these questions before finding out about the artistic approach to photography. How annoying it would be to see a good view and not know how to set the camera!

What are **settings**? There are really only two things you can 'set'. One is the amount of exposure; the other is the focus.

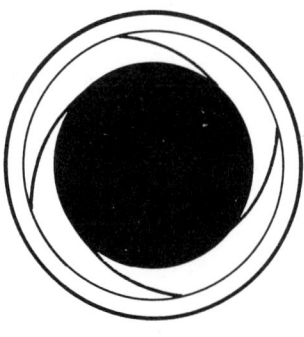

f/4

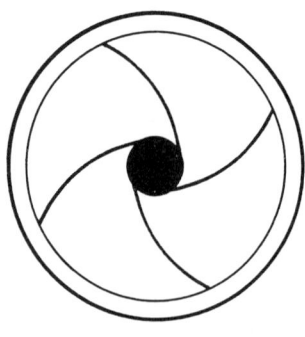

f/22

Getting the exposure right

The exposure setting allows you to get the right amount of light on to the film whether the day is dull or bright. Think back to when you were making prints on paper in daylight. When the light was very bright (perhaps in the sun) the paper darkened quite quickly. On a dull day you had to leave the printing frame out for a good while longer. A certain 'amount' of light had to fall on the paper before it went dark enough to make a print. A bright day and a short time, or a dull day and a long time. Either way, the final picture on the paper looked the same.

Camera lenses and shutters work in the same way, except that your film does not change colour in the *camera*. The image appears when the film is placed in a *photographic developer*. However, too much *or* too little light getting on the film in the camera, and you will not produce a properly exposed negative.

You have a lens, but the light cannot get through it on to the film because there is a **shutter** in the way. When you press the button (shutter release) you allow the shutter to open for a fraction of a second.

To allow the 'correct' amount of light to get on to the film, you can either vary the size of hole in the lens (**aperture**), or the time for the light to get through (**shutter speed**). Remember your daylight prints. Bright day – short time; dull day – longer time. In both cases the print looked the same. This is what exposure settings allow: either a lot of light getting through the lens for a short time, or less light for a longer time. What is important is to get the right 'quantity' of light on the film. Imagine you are filling a bucket with water from a tap. With the tap full on (like a lens at a wide aperture) you fill the bucket in a short time. With the tap on at a trickle (like a small lens aperture) you need a long time before the bucket is full.

Why bother with settings at all? Some simple cameras have no settings and they seem to work! They do, but only in bright weather. If you want to use a simple camera on dull days, you have to use a film that is more sensitive to light (a fast film).

Instead, it would be very nice to be able to open the lens aperture and so allow more light to pass through. Or you might choose to slow the shutter speed down, and allow more time for the light to get on to the film. 'Settings' are meant to help you take photographs in all sorts of different situations, but it is perfectly possible to take good views on bright days with a camera that has no 'settings' at all.

Shutter speed and aperture setting rings on a 35 mm camera

> Films are given a **speed rating**. The higher the number, the more sensitive the film is to light. For the moment remember that with a simple camera a medium speed film is suitable for bright days, and high speed films are essential for dull days. If your camera has a range of settings, you can use either type of film.

Photographing houses and views

What makes a good view? You stand on top of a high hill and see marvellous scenery far below. You take a photograph. Somehow the result is disappointing. Those fields and lanes that looked like a picture map are just an indistinct fuzzy area. The photograph makes them look too far away to be interesting any more.

The best scenery for photography is much closer to the camera. A field or lane that is near enough to be seen clearly. A gate or wall close to the camera gives added depth to the picture. A person or animal will give life. If you go to your local art gallery you won't see views from mountain tops unless there is plenty of detail in the foreground.

Setting the focusing

Of course, you don't need to go to the country to find suitable views. A bridge over a river in town, a tree in the park, and, of course, your house make a good picture. But don't forget to include something close to the camera to give depth. If your camera has no **focus adjustment** you point the camera and press the shutter. If you can adjust the focusing, where should it be set? The distance or the foreground? The answer is – the main point of interest. If you want the house to be clear, you won't mind if the

Box

roses close to the camera are not in focus! If you want the roses to be clear, you may not mind if the house is fuzzy.

Setting the aperture

This is where aperture settings are an advantage. The smaller the lens aperture (the higher the number), the more you will get sharply in focus, from close to far away. You may want both the house *and* the roses in focus. Of course, if you make the aperture smaller, not as much light will be getting to the film. To compensate for this you must slow down the shutter and allow the light longer to expose the film.

> A wide-aperture lens does not necessarily work better than a small-aperture lens. Its main advantage is the amount of light it will pass on a dull day. It will almost certainly be more expensive! If your lens has no apertures marked, it is possible to find out what they are. You will find out how to do this at the end of this chapter. Some simple cameras may have two or three aperture settings not marked with aperture numbers. They may have weather symbols instead.

Apertures are usually shown as a fraction. E.g. f/16: f is the focal length; f (the focal length) divided by 16. This gives you the measured diameter of the aperture. Other examples of aperture numbers are 8 and 11. Call them f8, f11, f16 and write them f/8, f/11 and f/16 and forget the theory if you want to.

Setting the shutter speed

Shutter speeds usually have a range: perhaps 1/30, 1/60 and 1/125. If there is no setting for shutter speeds you can assume yours will be around 1/30–1/60 second. If you are unable to discover the aperture of a simple camera, it is probably around f/11 or f/16.

Why have aperture settings as well as shutter speeds? Isn't it sufficient to alter only one according to the weather? If you want to make the most of your hobby, you have to be in charge of the camera, to choose the sort of result you get. A small aperture will give you plenty in focus. But you may not want plenty in focus! You may want to isolate a flower or person from the background. To do this you will need a wide aperture (and accurate focusing). A wide aperture will let too much light on to the film on a bright day, so unless you can alter the shutter speed to compensate for the opening of the aperture, you will have to wait for a dull day, or re-load the camera with a slow film – otherwise the exposure will be wrong.

Now suppose something is moving fast. You may want to 'freeze' it in action with a high shutter speed. You will then need to alter the aperture to correct the amount of light reaching the film. So, you see, sometimes you may want to choose a particular aperture, and other times a shutter speed, and you will have to alter the other one accordingly.

f/8 or f/11 are good general apertures that will give you plenty of the subject in focus. 1/125 or 1/60 of a second are generally accepted as 'normal' shutter speeds. If you slow your shutter speed below 1/25 or 1/30 of a second, you will find it very difficult to hold the camera steady. **Camera shake** is a nuisance and can spoil an otherwise good photograph. If the day is dull and you cannot open the aperture any further to allow a higher shutter speed, you can use a faster speed film; otherwise you must rest the camera on something. You do not necessarily need a tripod. If you can lean against a wall, or rest your elbows, you will find it much easier to hold the camera steady. Or you can rest the camera on a wall, or a fence.

Many people find it difficult to hold a camera steady even at speeds higher than 1/30 of a second. When your camera is empty, practise pressing the shutter while looking into a mirror. You will see if the camera jerks as you press the shutter. Folding cameras are among the most difficult to hold steady. Keep practising until you can press the shutter smoothly. Hold your breath as you start to press, and go on squeezing until you hear the click. Don't swing the camera away as soon as the picture is taken. You might misjudge when the shutter has actually fired.

Looking into a mirror will also tell you if you are in danger of photographing your thumb! I will not attempt to tell you how to hold a camera. If it feels comfortable and doesn't jerk when you press the shutter, you are probably holding it correctly. Different people will find different ways more comfortable.

To sum up about views and houses:

1. Find the correct exposure setting.
2. Decide on your combination of shutter speed and aperture.
3. Set the focusing for main point of interest (or a little closer if you are using a small aperture and want something in the foreground to be in focus as well).
4. Hold the camera upright or the verticals will lean.

5. Is there any way you could add more life or depth to the picture?
6. Hold your breath and squeeze the shutter gently.
7. Wind on the film for the next exposure.

If you have plenty of spare film, you could try taking a whole film just of views and houses. Try some photographs into the sun, but avoid dark shadows on large areas of buildings. The sun shining across the front of a building will show up the texture of the building material very well.

When you have finished the film, take it along for processing as before. When you get your negatives back, you will now be able to make daylight prints from them, or let the shop make prints if the negatives are good enough. If you are making your own prints, don't forget to ask for 'Process Only'.

Further information on shutter speeds, apertures and film speeds

Pass on to the next chapter if you do not want to read this section yet.

Shutter speeds

The way the shutter speeds are expressed is easy to understand. The time which the shutter is open is electronically measured at the factory. The shutter may have several **speeds** marked, and these are usually in fractions of a second. 8, 15, 30, 60, 125 are *fractions* of a second – 1/8, 1/15, 1/30, 1/60, 1/125 – but there is not usually room on the shutter to mark them as fractions. With a range of shutter speeds you have plenty of control over the time the image made by the lens can affect (expose) the film.

Apertures

The lens will have a metal hole in the middle which can be varied in size. Remember we are talking about cameras with a range of settings. This will probably have markings that go 4, 5.6, 8, 11, 16, 22. As the number gets higher, the hole in the lens gets smaller. This hole is called the

aperture but the metal part is an **iris**. This allows you to vary the **intensity** (brightness) of the light getting onto the film.

Measuring apertures

The **aperture number** is obtained by dividing the diameter of the aperture into the focal length of the lens. Here is how to find the aperture number of an unmarked lens. Measure the aperture (hole) as accurately as you can. If the lens is in the way, hold a ruler across the top and sight down by moving your head along to take the measurement from each side of this hole. Work to the nearest millimetre.

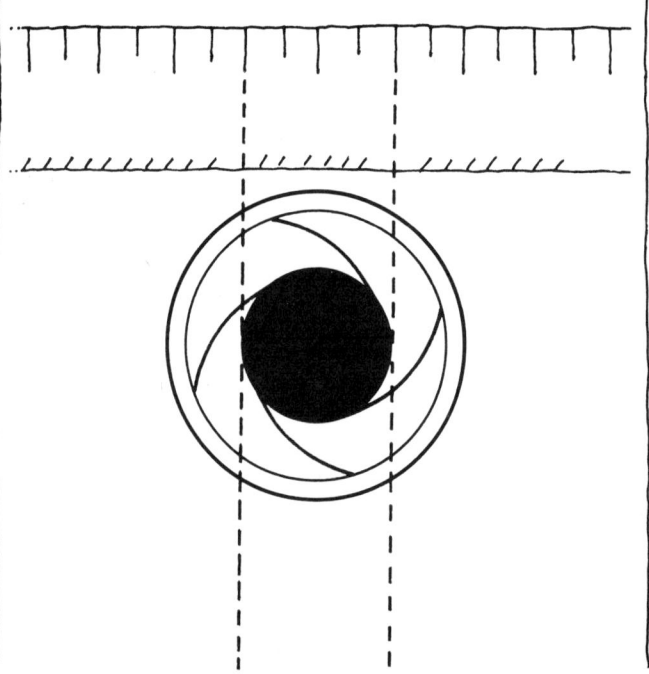

Now turn the camera on its side and adjust the focus to the infinity (far distance) setting. If the focus cannot be adjusted, it will be set correctly anyway. Now estimate where the centre of the lens is, and measure from there to the back of the camera (or film). Again, measure to the nearest millimetre.

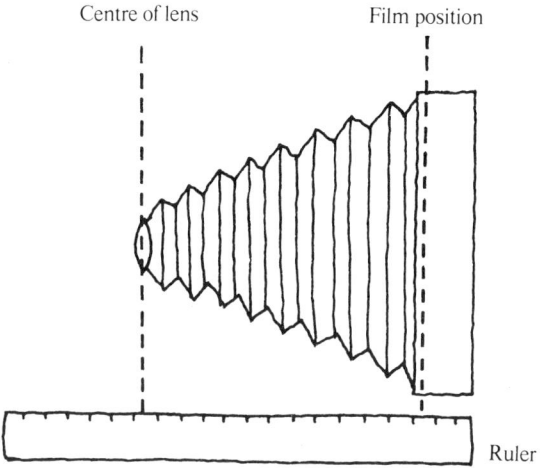

Divide the first measurement (diameter of the aperture) into the last measurement (length of camera). The result is the f number (aperture number) and it will probably be near one of the standard aperture markings. Now change the aperture and measure again.

Focal length

When a camera is focused on infinity, the distance between the centre of the lens and the film is the **focal length** of the lens. At least, it is with most cameras. Single-lens reflex cameras have a special design of lens to allow the viewing mirror to be fitted into the camera body. The lens may be further away from the film than its focal length would suggest. However, single-lens reflex lenses all have their apertures clearly marked. Perhaps your camera only has a couple of weather symbols to mark the aperture settings. It is very useful to know what apertures they are.

Changing the settings

An exposure guide packed with the film will not give a *range* of shutter speeds and apertures for you to choose from. At this stage you can make your own. The aperture numbers halve or double the amount of light getting to the film as they go up or down. Don't forget, the higher the number, the smaller the hole, so the less light gets through. Here is a long range of aperture markings. You will not have them all on your lens:

1.4, 2, 2.8, 4, 5.6, 8, 11, 16, 22, 32, 45, 64

The lowest number you have will be your lens's widest aperture. The wider this is, the easier it will be to work in dull light.

To work out your own exposure tables for different shutter speeds and apertures you need to understand the connection between shutter speeds and apertures. If the correct exposure is 1/125 of a second at an aperture of f/11, you may want to alter the aperture. (You find out the correct exposure by using the guide with the film, or an exposure meter.) If you alter the aperture from f/11 to f/16, less light will be getting to the film. You can correct this by slowing the shutter speed down from 1/125 to 1/60 of a second. Modern shutter speeds and apertures are both worked out to double or halve the light getting to the film.

If you want to use a higher shutter speed to stop movement, you might use 1/250 of a second instead of 1/125. In which case, what aperture setting would you have to use? You started with f/11, so you must open up one **stop** to f/8. These aperture numbers are usually known as **stops**.

Film speeds

The most popular film speed is called the **ASA** rating (American Standards Association). An **ASA** rating of 100–160 would be called medium speed. If the **ASA** number is doubled, the film speed will then be twice as fast. A high speed (or fast) film will have an **ASA** rating of about 400. If you double this number, you double the speed rating. If you halve this number, you halve the speed rating – and the speed rating shows the film's sensitivity to light.

Different film speeds introduce another variable. You can alter shutter speeds, apertures *and* film speeds. Once the camera is loaded with film you can only adjust shutter speeds and apertures.

An experiment

If you have some spare film you could try taking one exposure at your camera's widest aperture (with a high shutter speed) and another identical shot at the camera's smallest aperture with a slow shutter speed.

If you get the exposure right both times, then the negatives will appear identical at first sight. However, there will be a difference which you will understand better after reading the next chapter. The difference will be in the amount of subject that is sharply in focus.

4 Focusing and people

This chapter is about photographing people and animals. Find the print of people you made from your first film. Perhaps the picture is not perfect. More than likely the background is quite sharply in focus, but the people look rather fuzzy. In fact, they are out of focus. The camera lens 'thought' it was looking at the far distance.

Of course the camera lens can't really think, although a few expensive automatic models go some way towards this. You have to 'tell' the lens what part of the picture you require sharply in focus. You can do this by measuring the distance from the camera to the subject, and then setting that distance on the lens.

Suppose your camera has no focus adjustment? For the time being, you had better be content with making sure the person you are photographing is at least two metres away. Later on, you will be able to get as close as you like, using close-up lenses. If you already know how to use these, go ahead straight away.

Depth of field

It is easy to get too anxious about setting the focusing distance exactly. We'll say that the person is two metres from the camera. Exactly two metres. You set the focus to two metres. If the focusing scale on the camera is correct, then you can be sure the person will be in focus. Suppose they step back a very small distance – say ten millimetres. Will they still be in focus? Ten millimetres? Of course, you say, ten millimetres is almost nothing. Suppose they step back twenty millimetres? Yes, probably. Thirty millimetres? Forty? Fifty? Perhaps.

But there has to be a point when you would look at a print and decide the person was no longer sharply in focus. Now suppose they move forward. How far? Again there will come a distance when you can say they are no longer sharply in focus. This distance each side of the point where you focus is called the **depth of field**. It is the depth between the nearest point sharply in focus and the farthest.

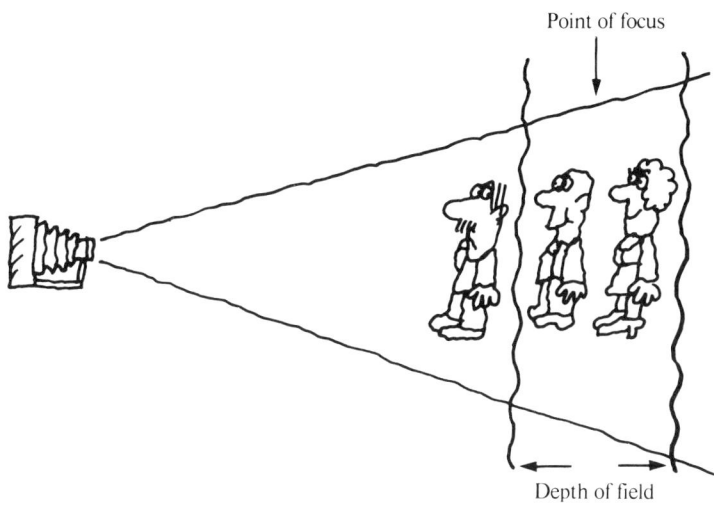

Point of focus

Depth of field

A small lens has greater depth of field than a large lens. This is why small cameras often have no focusing adjustment, yet the picture is sharp from the far distance to perhaps as close as one metre on a sunny day. On a sunny day, of course, you will be able to use a small aperture – and small apertures give a greater depth of field.

When photographing people you usually want to be quite close. If your camera has no focusing adjustment, you must find out the closest you can come and still keep the person in sharp focus. Here is a reasonable estimate of this closest distance with simple cameras. This table is worked out for an aperture of about f/16.

Large box camera	2–3 metres
Square box camera	2 metres
126 Cartridge-loading camera	1.5 metres
110 Cartridge-loading camera	1 metre

One thing to bear in mind. The larger the camera (longer focal length lens), the more careful you have to be about focusing. The zone in which the person can move backwards and forwards (depth of field) gets less as the focal length increases – or as you open the aperture wider.

Photographing people (*photo no. 3*)

You may not have been able to understand all that has been said about this, in which case try reading it again later. In any case, you are supposed to be taking a photograph of a friend! It often helps if you can get your friends to sit down while you are taking their photographs. Some people will feel very awkward when they are standing. They are not sure where to hold their hands, or whether to stand with their feet apart or together. While they are worrying about this, they are hardly likely to look relaxed! Besides, you may find that you want to keep checking the settings on your camera. If your friend gets tired, he or she may decide to go and do something else. Give them a book or magazine to look at. This should help take their minds off the ordeal!

And what should *you* be doing? Make your camera settings beforehand. You should make sure the background is suitable. No drain-pipes growing out of the top of your friend's head? No speckly shadows? Remember, the background will be as much a part of the photograph as your friend. It has to be *right*.

Is *everything* right? Are you sure? The focusing set as accurately as you can reasonably estimate? Then say something to attract your friend's attention. As they look up – click! There, with a bit of luck, will be a good photograph. (Don't get too close though. If you go too close, your friend will look strange with a very long

35 mm

Where you (the photographer) stand can make or spoil the picture

nose.) I won't say 'portrait' because I think of portraits as needing a bit extra in the way of lighting. This extra lighting will give a roundness (or modelling) to the face which lifts it out of the snapshot category. Make no mistake, though, some ordinary photographs look far more like the person than many studio portraits do. Next time you are near a portrait photographer's studio, look at the window display. See if you can work out the 'something' that makes them 'portraits' and not just 'photographs'.

One thing that is difficult to achieve in a studio is a sense of activity. To record action you need to create the impression that you are looking at part of a much longer action. You can see that something has *been* happening, *this* is happening now, and the action will *continue* naturally. This is the effect to aim for.

Imagine two or three children talking. You come along with your camera and tell them you want to take their photograph. What do they do? They line up and put on big smiles. Where is the action now? Suppose you could come along invisibly and as their conversation continues you press the shutter. There, in

T.L.R.

the photograph, will be a split second of their life. You can look at the picture and try and imagine what they were talking about. There is no line-up with foolish grins. It is a moment of life that has *been* going on, is happening *now*, and will seem to go on after the photograph has been put down.

You do not need a high shutter speed for this sort of 'action' photograph, but you do need to practise with an *empty* camera and a mirror. Make all the settings and then hold the camera at your side. Use a full-length mirror. Without looking, point the camera at the place where you guess your reflection is. Now you can look. Is the camera pointing in the right direction? Turn the other way and try again. Now press the shutter. Gain confidence in this way with the empty camera and then go out into the park or street with film. Make sure you do not upset anyone. You may not be quite as 'invisible' as you think!

It may be possible to buy a mirror attachment to fit over the front of your lens. This looks out at right-angles so people don't think the camera is being pointed at them! Many years ago, when films became fast enough to allow pictures to be taken without a tripod, several strange 'secret' cameras were made. One fitted inside a hat, and another in a small case. Yet another was disguised as a pocket watch. Nowadays spies seem to have them in wristwatches and cigarette lighters if we are to believe what we see in films. Can you hide your camera inside an unsuspicious package?

Twin-lens reflex cameras are excellent for this sort of photography – usually called **candid photography**. You can hold the camera sideways, but pretend you are taking something directly

T.L.R.

in front of you. You will need to keep looking up in front, and not to the side, to complete the deception.

Whether you are catching people unawares, or your friends when they are relaxed enough to forget you are holding a camera pointed at them, this is the best way of photographing people looking natural. I'm sure you will understand if I repeat my warning: do not make a nuisance of yourself, and make sure that the person you are photographing is not likely to be upset if they find out!

Action photo

That is one way of capturing action. Now, what about the runner? You may have seen pictures of the start of a race. The runners are leaving their starting blocks, and their muscles are taut. They seem to be 'frozen' in their tracks. This type of photography calls for a very high shutter speed. Perhaps 1/2000 of a second. You can 'freeze' anything if the exposure is short enough.

No photograph can ever really convey the fantastic speed of a racing car as it shoots past the photographer. If the camera shutter speed is too fast, you will make the car look as if it's parked. And what sort of action picture would that be?

An experienced photographer will swing his camera round and follow the car. At the same time, he will press the shutter but keep moving the camera. The photograph will show a car sharply in focus, but the background will be a streaked blur. The slower the shutter speed, the greater the amount of the blur, and so the greater impression of speed. Of course, you have to be careful to swing the camera to follow the racing car exactly, or both car and background will be blurred. If the photographer holds the camera still, the *background* will be sharp, and the *car* will come out as a blur.

We're not photographing racing cars in this chapter, but people. If a friend runs past the camera, you can swing the camera to follow him. Try it, but don't press the shutter yet. There is no need for him to run very fast. Don't use a very high shutter

35 mm

35 mm

Same bicycle speed but different shutter speeds. The first photograph was taken at 1/250 of a second, and the lower one at 1/30. In both cases the camera was being swung to follow the movement

speed or you will lose the impression of movement. Simple cameras have a fixed shutter speed of about 1/30 of a second. If you are careful, this is quite fast enough.

Have a few practice swings, and then press the shutter. It is very important to keep following the movement, even after you have pressed the shutter. If you don't, you may find that you stop swinging the camera just a fraction of a second *before* you take the picture.

If you have been lucky, your first photograph will show a blurred background and a sharp runner, but not sharp arms and legs. This is because the arms and legs do not move in exactly the same direction and at the same speed as the body. It is obvious when you think about it. Don't see this as a failure. The picture opposite was taken in the park with an old box camera.

You may have found it difficult to swing the camera in time with the person running. If you are having to look down into a small viewfinder it may be almost impossible to follow the runner. The box camera used for the photograph had a wire frame viewfinder that swung up on to the front. You could make a viewfinder

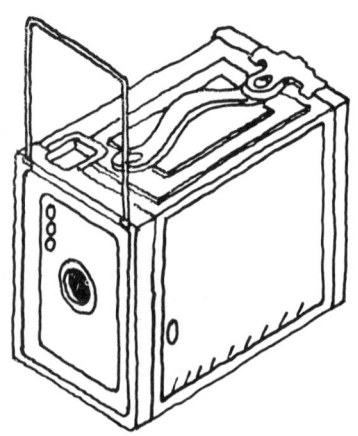

Box

like this for your camera if you need one. All you need to do is to bend a wire frame large enough to show the same area of view as the camera viewfinder.

If your camera is empty, then just practise pressing the shutter as you swing round. You will find it takes quite a bit of practice to do this smoothly. This type of picture is best rehearsed. Make sure your friend runs along the edge of a path or line. You can measure the distance to this line and set your focusing accurately.

To sum up:

1. You shouldn't freeze action if you want the picture to look alive.
2. Photograph people when they are not thinking about the camera.
3. Watch the background!

Animals

If you want to photograph animals, start with your own or other people's pets. Wild animals are too difficult to approach, and you must either build a hide or use a remote trip device to work the shutter. Zoo animals can't get away – hopefully! – but bars and cages usually get in the way of the camera.

Pets are best kept amused by a friend. Try tying a small piece of stick to some dark thread, then pulling it through the grass to attract your pet's attention. The stick will not look out of place in the photograph, and the thread will not show up – unless you have an especially good lens. Let your friend pull the thread until your pet comes into the right position to be photographed. Then whistle or call. As soon as your pet looks up, *take the picture!* That alert, slightly surprised look is what makes an interesting photograph.

If that fails, an animal waking up or eating is fairly certain to

The sky makes a quick and easy background. There is nothing to distract the eye from the subject

stay in place long enough for at least one photograph. Do try and get all your settings made in advance, and be prepared to give up and try again later. Some animals seem determined to be awkward whenever there is a camera around! Don't forget the background. It is as important with animals as it is with people.

You could combine a picture of a pet and a friend. Instead of having them both sitting (or standing) and looking at the camera, get a photograph of them playing together. If a dog is jumping up for food, try and take the photograph exactly at the *top* of the jump. In this way the dog will not be moving and so will come

110
Cartridge

If there are bars or wires in the way, then this is the best you can expect. Instead, try photographing the less dangerous animals where you can either place the *lens* between the wire, or look over the top

out sharply (clearly). If you can manage this, then you've begun to master 'timing', and timing is what is needed for getting good action photographs.

At the zoo you can put the camera lens right up against the wire of a cage – but first make sure that the occupant of the cage is not dangerous! Glass in the reptile house will help steady the camera for slow shutter speeds. Wherever you are, always steady the camera if possible. Unless you can get your camera looking *between* bars or wire netting, you won't get a good photograph. You will see the bars or wires clearly, and the animal or bird will tend to be hidden.

That should be enough information to help you get started. If you want to specialize in animal photography, I suggest you get a book on the subject. I have chosen eight different photographs for the assignments in this book and by the time you have finished reading it, you may have decided to become as expert

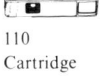
110 Cartridge

Even a clear view is no guarantee of a good photo. The background is terrible. The coatimondi is almost invisible, and whose is that tail?

as possible in just one of the eight subjects. However, the experience gained in the other seven will be invaluable!

Your pet may be very small, or your camera may not focus for anything much smaller than elephants! In Chapter 7 you will find out how to get over this focusing problem. You can read Chapter 7 straight away if you want to get on with animal photography in close-up, but if you can wait until you have read the next chapter, you may find close-up photography easier to understand.

110
Cartridge

Once again the sky is used. No bars, no background, Just two coatimondis playing. Not as exciting as lions but a more interesting photo

Further information on focusing and depth of field

You can pass straight on to the next chapter if you do not want to become involved in the technicalities at this stage.

How to focus

To get things close to the camera in focus, you have to move the lens away from the film. To focus on distant objects, you bring the lens closer to the film. If your camera has focus settings, you can probably watch it happen. (Some simple cameras have a close-up lens that fits in front of the camera lens to allow photographs to be taken near to the camera.) Some lenses are focused by turning just the front part. This alters the focusing by changing the focal length of the lens. Even so, the front part of the lens moves backwards and forwards, but not very noticeably.

Depth of field

Depth of field will vary from lens to lens, and from aperture to aperture. The smaller the aperture, the greater the depth of field. Also, the smaller the camera, the greater the depth of field. How can that be?

Do you remember in the last chapter I told you how to measure the focal length of a lens? You set the focus on the far distance (infinity), and measured from the centre of the lens to the back of the camera. It might be as much as 150 mm. That is a long distance, and such a camera is probably large. Or perhaps the distance is 75 mm. Most twin-lens reflex and square box cameras have lenses of 75 mm focal length. 35 mm and 126 Instamatic-type cameras might have 40, 45 or 50 mm focal length lenses. 110 cartridge cameras are around 25 mm. In most cases this focal length will be marked on the lens mount.

Standard lenses

Why all these different focal lengths? I expect you have heard of wide-angle and telephoto lenses. If a lens is neither wide-angle nor telephoto, it is called a **normal** or **standard** lens. If you measure across the diagonal of a negative, you will find that the measurement is close to that of the focal length of your lens. So, a normal (or standard) lens is approximately the same focal length as the diagonal measurement of your negative. As different cameras have different film sizes, so they each have a focal length of lens to suit. A standard lens of 40 mm for a small camera will include the same view as a 150 mm standard lens on a much larger camera. A large negative needs a large picture to fill it.

Depth of field again

To return to depth of field. The smaller the hole (aperture) in your lens, the greater the depth of field. Since the aperture is the focal length divided by the diameter of this hole, it follows that f/8 on a 50 mm lens is a smaller hole than f/8 on a 150 mm focal length lens. This may not have occurred to you before but it makes sense when you think about it. A camera lens is rather like a projector. It projects a picture of what is outside, on to a film inside the camera. If the lens is looking at a car parked across the road, how bright that car is on your film depends on the diameter of the hole (aperture) in your lens. But a lens with a long focal length has to be further away from the film than a lens with a 50 mm focal length. Remember, the focal length is the distance from the lens to the film when it is focused on the far distance.

If f/8 was the same diameter hole in each lens, the 150 mm focal length lens would not be projecting such a bright picture, and that would make nonsense of

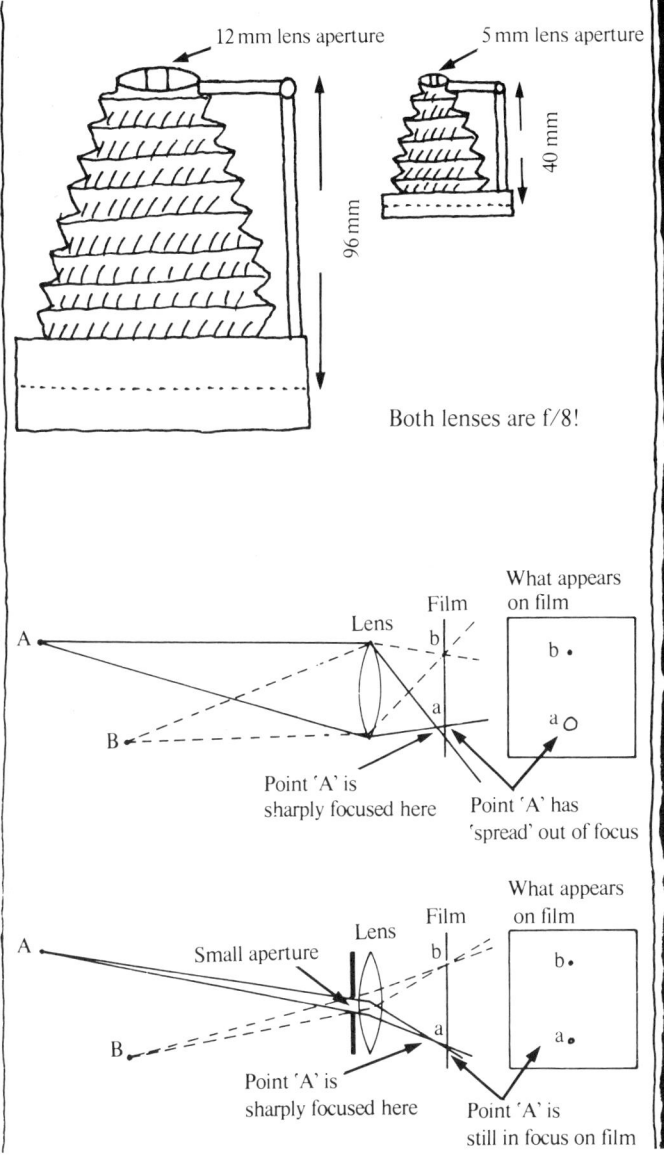

12 mm lens aperture 5 mm lens aperture

96 mm 40 mm

Both lenses are f/8!

Lens — Film — What appears on film

Point 'A' is sharply focused here Point 'A' has 'spread' out of focus

Small aperture

Point 'A' is sharply focused here Point 'A' is still in focus on film

apertures. f/8 *must* be able to pass the same amount of light whatever the focal length of the lens.

These illustrations show why a large aperture has a very limited depth of field. Only 'Point B' is in focus at 'b' in the first drawing. In the second, the camera is still focused on 'Point B'. However, the rays of light from 'Point A' are narrow because they have passed through a small aperture. Even though the exact focus for 'Point A' is in front of the film, 'Point A' will appear to be in focus. The rays of light have spread slightly, but not enough to spoil the picture. This is how **depth of field** works.

You may sometimes hear this called the **depth of focus**, but depth of focus refers to the amount you can alter the distance between the lens and the film in your camera and still keep the subject sharply in focus. This might be a millimetre, or even less. Since you are unlikely to hear much about depth of focus in its true sense, you can usually assume that most people mean depth of field when they say depth of focus. Only when you get on to more advanced photography is it important to realize that there is a difference.

5 All sorts of cameras

Although there are many different makes and models of cameras, there are only a few basic *types*. There is no such thing as the perfect camera, but some are better suited to certain jobs than others. To take on a wide range of work, a professional photographer would need several cameras and lenses. But at the moment it is not vitally important to you that *every* photograph should be the best possible.

I am going to describe the main types of camera in some detail. I imagine you will be able to find one which is fairly close to your own. I'm going to start with the most expensive and most complicated to use, and go on through to the simplest cameras. Don't worry if yours is at the end of the list! These will be the cheapest to buy, and it is quite a challenge to get the sort of results which you would normally expect from the more expensive models.

The monorail camera

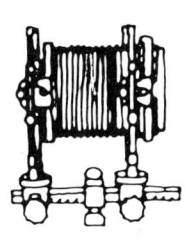 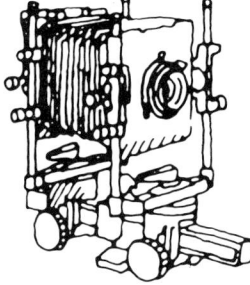 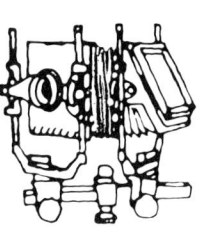

This camera is expensive to buy, expensive to run and difficult to operate. Definitely not a camera for the beginner! You clamp this camera on a tripod and look through it with a black cloth over your head. Properly used it is capable of some of the finest work ever produced. You may think it looks old-fashioned, and in a way it is. It is a very basic shape. A lens at the front, film at the back and something joining the two to keep the light off the film. But then that's what all cameras are like.

The difference between a monorail and a conventional camera is the way it is used. I'll describe very briefly how it works. If you find it difficult to understand it may make more sense if you go back and re-read this section when you have finished the whole book.

The lens covers a wide view, but the negative in the back of the camera only uses part of the picture available. If you want to include the top of a high building you do not need to tip the camera upwards. Doing that only makes the walls of the building appear to lean inwards as they go up. I'm sure you've seen that happen! You keep the monorail camera level and raise the front panel with the lens. That puts a 'new' part of the picture on the film, and the 'new' part contains the top of the building. Of course, you have to be far enough back to make sure the bottom of the building is still in the picture. You know exactly what will be in the picture because under the black cloth you can see the picture projected upside down on to a focusing screen. When you are satisfied with the set-up, you place a film holder into the back of the camera and make the exposure. That one piece of film can now be processed or kept until later. You can take a colour picture followed immediately by black-and-white if you have film holders loaded with sheets of different films.

If you want to focus on very close objects, the lens has to be moved further away from the film. This is no problem. You slide the two panels away from each other on the rail, and the flexible bellows expand to allow this to happen. That now brings us on to another interesting feature. If an object is far away from the camera, the lens has to be brought closer to the film to make sure it is in focus (sharp). Imagine two objects at different distances from the camera. The one close to the camera will require the lens far away from the film for it to be in focus. The further object will require the lens to be closer to the film. If you look at these illustrations, you will discover some interesting facts about focusing, as well as monorail cameras.

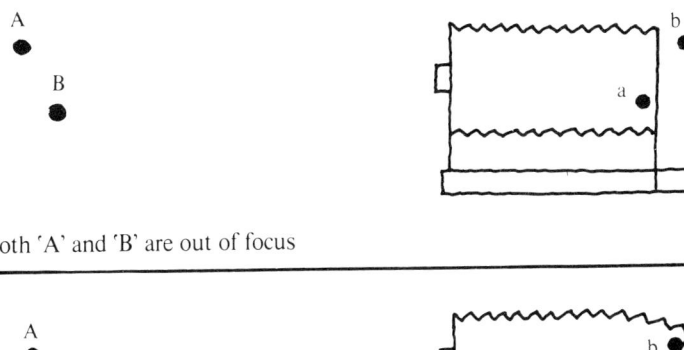

Both 'A' and 'B' are out of focus

Camera back tilted to allow 'A' and 'B' to be in focus

Do you see how the film can be tipped back to get both objects in focus? That would be impossible with most types of camera. There are many other 'tricks' you can do with a monorail camera so it is an essential piece of equipment for some types of photography. It is extremely unlikely that you will be using one, but out of interest let's see how well it would have performed on your list of assignments in Chapter 1.

House and view. A monorail camera is not always suitable for outside work. It can be shaken by the wind for one thing. It is at its best in a studio. However, there is much to be said for the way you do not need to tip the camera up or down to get all a building included, so it would have come out of this test very well – but only in experienced hands.

People out of doors. There is no viewfinder on a monorail camera. You focus on a ground glass screen. If you can set up the camera in advance and pose people, then it can be used, but it would not be a first choice unless giant-size enlargements were required from the very large negative produced. People running would be very difficult to manage.

Animals. You will find that the problems that existed when trying to photograph people are even greater, though there would be no problem in focusing close enough.

Toys and models. An excellent camera. You can take your time with the focusing and use the camera **movements** to the full. (**Movements** are the many parts of the camera that move.) Given enough time, almost anyone could get the camera set up correctly. No excuses for out-of-focus pictures here!

Insects and flowers. Excellent again, as long as the subject is not moving. Very inconvenient trying to follow a moving insect around a flower!

People indoors. Difficult to use when people are involved. With cameras of this type exposure times are usually long because they are used at small apertures. Sometimes this type of camera is used to photograph people in a bright studio to get very high quality results for advertising. In poor room lighting the exposure time would be too long for people to stand still.

Single-lens reflex camera

A single-lens reflex camera is the ultimate dream for many photographers. There is a mirror behind the lens. When you look into the viewfinder, you look into the mirror and out through the lens. Thus you see exactly what the lens is seeing. When the picture is sharply focused in the viewfinder, the picture will be sharply focused on the negative. When you press the shutter release, the mirror swings up out of the way and allows the picture to be taken.

Single-lens reflex cameras come in many sizes, and work in various ways. The majority take 35 mm film. What they share in common is the viewfinder which works directly through the lens. If you fit a wide-angle or telephoto lens, you see the new picture in the viewfinder. If you come very close to the subject, you see exactly how much is in the picture, and can adjust the focusing very accurately. There are several cheap single-lens reflex cameras on the market as well as models costing several hundred pounds. The cheaper models usually lack certain features which *may* annoy you as your interest in photography grows. It will pay you to take great care in selecting a suitable model if you buy a single-lens reflex (usually called an S.L.R.).

House and view. If you have a choice of wide-angle and telephoto lenses you will be able to choose better view-points for many houses and landscapes. The viewfinder will show you exactly what the final picture will be like. If you are tipping the camera up or down, you will notice the uprights leaning inwards or outwards.

People standing and running. An S.L.R. would be an unnecessary luxury here. No excuses for not doing a good job! However, there are some people who would argue that an S.L.R. is not very good for following moving people, which just goes to show that there is not an ideal camera for everyone.

Animals. Focusing close enough for animals would be easy with any S.L.R. The cheaper ones may not be so easy to use for following a lively animal. The lens may have to be opened up to wide aperture for focusing and then set to a smaller aperture for the exposure. It may be difficult to follow the subject at this smaller aperture and tell if it is still sharply in focus. Most models will stop down automatically to the selected aperture the instant you press the shutter release. This allows you to see the focusing screen always at full aperture.

Toys and models. The closer you get to your subject with a camera, the more you realize just how useful an S.L.R. is. Focusing is no problem. You can screw a close-up lens in front of your camera lens. Or, if the camera lens is removable, you can fit extension tubes between the camera lens and the camera body. These extension tubes take the lens further away from the film, and focus the camera very close to the subject. Different lengths of extension tubes allow various working distances.

Insects, etc. If your camera allows you to focus at the lens's widest aperture and stops itself down automatically when you press the shutter release, it will be easy to follow a moving insect. In any case, an S.L.R. must be near one hundred per cent perfect for this sort of work.

People indoors. Ordinary room lighting is not very bright. If you want to hold your camera in your hand, the lens will have to be used at its widest aperture. Accurate focusing is essential if you are photographing at wide apertures. Viewing through the lens allows you to focus accurately and quickly. If you are taking portraits, a telephoto lens can be fitted. You can work from further away and still fill the negative with the head and shoulders of your friend.

Twin-lens reflex camera

Sometimes called a T.L.R. camera. A T.L.R. is usually as expensive to buy new as a single-lens reflex but they are a better buy second-hand. A T.L.R. is really two cameras on top of each other. The top lens is focused through a mirror on to a focusing screen. In this way it is similar to an S.L.R. However, the top lens is only for viewing. The bottom lens has the shutter and aperture setting. It focuses straight on to the film. The front panel holding the two lenses moves in and out for focusing. When one lens is in focus, so is the other. Twin-lens reflex cameras usually take roll films and so may be a bit more expensive to operate than a single-lens reflex camera (if the S.L.R. takes 35 mm film – and the majority do). However, most people find they get better quality prints from the larger negatives – but the camera is also larger, and perhaps more awkward to carry around. Let's see how well a twin-lens reflex would have performed on our assignment.

House and view. The large focusing screen (usually 60 mm by 60 mm) makes it easy to set the camera level and pointing in exactly the right direction. A T.L.R. will certainly cope well with houses and views. Looking down on to the focusing screen is like looking at a print of the picture you are taking – but, of course, in colour.

People. I like the twin-lens reflex as a reliable straightforward camera. There is very little that can go wrong. However, there is one feature that some photographers find hard to accept. The viewing screen reverses everything left to right. If you are holding the camera still, and a walking figure moves off the right-hand edge of the focusing screen, you have to swing the camera to the *left* to find them again. If you get a chance to look into a twin-lens reflex, you will understand what I mean. It *is* possible to get used to this. As a personal view, a twin-lens reflex offers the best value in cameras to the serious amateur photographer who has limited funds to spend on equipment. Some makes are not too expensive new, and even better value second-hand. They never seem to wear out. Their attraction is in their simplicity and high performance. Having said that, I have to point out that they need to be used carefully, and with some skill, to achieve good results. It is easy to focus on people, and the focusing screen helps you to compose good portraits.

Animals. Here is a good way of discovering the difficulties of a reversed focusing screen. Try following a lively dog about the garden for ten minutes! No problem about focusing close, though.

Toys and models. The two lenses present a bit of difficulty. You are unlikely to be able to focus closer than one metre without close-up lenses. When working at quite a distance from the subject, the two lenses are seeing near enough the same scene. However, the viewing lens *is* higher than the taking lens. When you get close to the subject, the viewing lens is seeing a higher part of the scene. It is possible to buy close-up lenses where the viewing one has a prism which turns the view down to match the taking lens. (With a T.L.R. you must have a close-up lens on both the viewing and the taking lens.) In Chapter 7 I will explain a way of using a twin-lens reflex as an S.L.R.

Insects, etc. The problem of having two separate viewing lenses becomes worse now. Twin-lens reflex cameras are not intended for this type of work – but don't let that put you off! Read Chapter 7.

People indoors. Not very good in ordinary room lighting. Lenses are not wide aperture. Quite easy to focus. There is one make with interchangeable lenses allowing telephoto and wide-angle lens panels to be fitted. Also another make with completely separate wide-angle and telephoto cameras. Expensive to buy, but some professionals are very keen on them.

Standard 35 mm

Under this heading we will have to include every 35 mm camera that isn't a single-lens reflex. They will range from the simplest model with settings made by moving a pointer to symbols of sun and clouds, to very expensive models with interchangeable lenses. Somewhere in between will be the type with a full range of shutter speeds and apertures, and others which are fully automatic in operation, requiring no setting other than focusing. The fully automatic models sound attractive to the complete beginner, but he may soon get fed up with having no controls to set. These

models will work excellently on most subjects, but there are bound to be occasions where a manually operated camera will give superior results. Some automatic cameras offer the best of both worlds – full automation and complete manual operation. There are very few new models available if you want a simple type, but a large number of second-hand. Choose a high quality make if you want a reliable second-hand model.

A 35 mm camera produces relatively small negatives which will need enlarging. However, this size of film is very convenient for taking colour slides. When you buy a camera, you will have to decide whether to take large high quality negatives on roll film, or colour slides and negatives on smaller film. Perhaps two cameras would be best! With 35 mm cameras you have to rewind the film into the cassette, inside the camera, before opening the camera back. Be warned!

Houses and views. Automatic cameras are excellent for this sort of work. No fiddling with settings. You see the view, you point the camera in the right direction and press the shutter. Easy. Some viewfinders will be easier to use than others. When buying second-hand, look for a **bright-line** viewfinder. When viewing, the subject is surrounded by an illuminated frame. It is easy to see the edges of the picture, and also some of the subject which is not going to be included in your photograph. Automatic, or manual 35 mm cameras are good for general use.

People standing and running. The same details apply here as above.

Animals. The same again! If you have a built-in **rangefinder** you will find accurate focusing easier.

Toys and models. You can fit a close-up lens, but the viewfinder will be viewing *above* the camera lens. This is the same problem twin-lens reflex cameras suffer from. Without a close-up lens attachment, you will not be able to get much closer than one metre. Unless you make allowances for the separation of the viewfinder and camera lens, you will cut the top off your subject at close range. Some viewfinders have a dotted line to mark the edge of the picture on close-ups.

Insects, etc. Even worse here. Problem can be overcome. Read Chapter 7.

People indoors. Some cameras have wide-aperture lenses. These can be used in room lighting. Fully automatic cameras usually show a 'not-sufficient-light' signal, and so have to be used with flash.

Cartridge loading

These will take either 126 or 110 film. 110 film is so small (16 mm wide) that it may not be worth processing and printing it yourself. If you have a 110 camera, keep reading, because you will be able to tackle most of these jobs with it. 126 and 110 cameras were introduced for the person who is only interested in getting results with the minimum of knowledge and fuss. 126 cartridges take film 35 mm in width, but without the perforations of

conventional 35 mm film running along each edge of the film. 126 film is processed and printed in the same way as 35 mm film.

The majority of cartridge-loading cameras are made with the minimum of settings. There are some with complex automation, and even a few cameras at the top end of the market for semi-professional use. The details that apply to 35 mm cameras will be the same for cartridge-loading models. Remember, though, that the majority of cartridge-loading cameras have no facility for setting a range of shutter speeds and apertures. The settings are often in weather symbols. Focusing is not usually possible but the depth of field is tremendous, especially with the 'pocket-sized' 110 models.

Folding cameras

Nearly all of these were designed to take roll film. I say 'were', because very very few are being manufactured nowadays. They may look old-fashioned, but can produce high quality results. Folding flat, they can be carried in a pocket or bag without being a nuisance. Unless you are buying from a well-trusted source, they *must* be checked over thoroughly. The folding bellows may leak light, the front lens panel may not be parallel to the film, and the focus settings may not be correct on the scale. This may all sound alarming. Unless you are able to try a film through the camera before handing over any money, allow sufficient cash for a complete overhaul.

Some folding models were very simple, and performed no

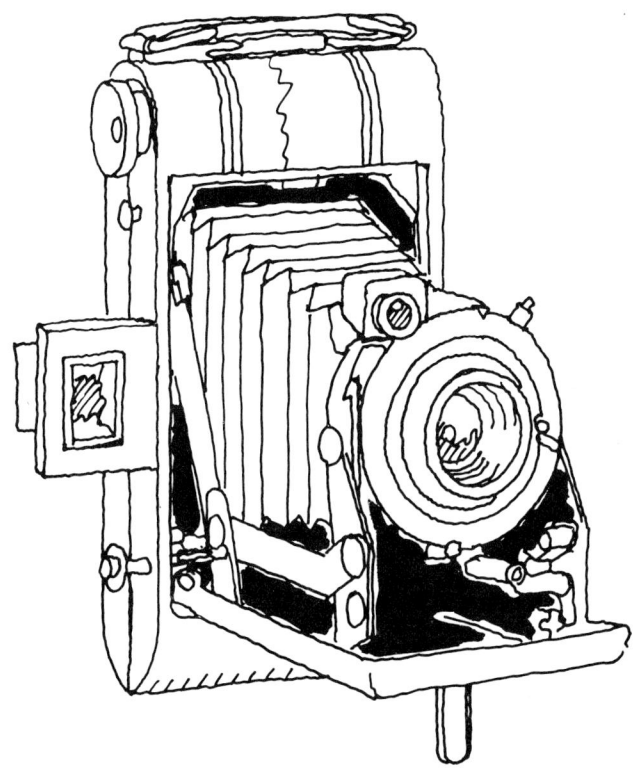

better than box cameras when *new*. Others were fitted with the very best lenses and shutters obtainable. Buy from a photographic dealer rather than a junk shop unless you feel sure you can tell a good model from a bad one – or unless the price is so low it is worth taking a chance. A *good* folding camera is the cheapest way for a beginner to equip himself and learn sound basic photography. No 'point-the-camera-and-press' automation here. Every setting has to be made, and focusing is especially important.

Houses and views. The viewfinders on the majority of folding cameras are small and difficult to see through clearly. The edges of the picture are difficult to detect with confidence. Older models have small focusing screens you look down on, and the later models have eye-level finders. You may be able to buy a large, eye-level finder which can be screwed or stuck on. These large viewfinders were available as accessories, and some shops may still have them in their drawer of odds-and-ends. With a small viewfinder, it will be difficult to get buildings and horizons straight. However, if you go back a bit further, you will have enough 'spare' picture to be able to straighten the part you want when printing the negative.

People standing and running. The larger lens of a folding camera requires more accurate focusing than the smaller lens of a 35 mm camera. (See page 61.) Apart from that, a folding camera will give results at least as good as a 35 mm model, and probably a lot better.

Animals. Again, focusing is important – even more so at close distances.

Toys and models. Without a close-up lens, you will not be able to come sufficiently close. If you keep one metre away, the object will look very small on the negative. If you ignore the focusing scale and just come close to the subject, the picture will be badly out of focus.

Insects, etc. As above, but worse still.

People indoors. One manufacturer in particular produced inexpensive folding cameras with wide-aperture lenses. With these you can hand-hold a camera at 1/30 second in ordinary room lighting by using a high speed film. Otherwise you need a longer exposure, brighter lights or flash. A lot of folding cameras are too old to have shutters which will work with flash, although they can be adapted.

Box cameras

I like box cameras. My first camera was a very old box camera. They are easy to use, extremely cheap to buy second-hand and very reliable. They were sold for making snap-shots only, so you may like the challenge of producing good results from every picture on your assignment! Don't be too quick to dismiss box cameras. A box camera will teach you a lot about photography, and there's a good chance you'll be able to find one of your relations who will give you his or her old one.

Your box camera pictures may all have failed, except those of the house and view. Not only will the viewfinder be small, the tiny mirror in the viewfinder system may have moved or become cloudy. And not many box cameras can be focused on close subjects.

You *can* get round most of these limitations. When you understand more fully how cameras work, you will be able to overcome their shortcomings. This picture was taken with a very ordinary box camera, and was not just a lucky shot. It could be repeated time and time again on models, insects or anything small. Now you will *have* to read on!

Box

An expensive camera in a studio? No, just a box camera, a hazy sun out of doors, and the sky as the background!

6 Dark-room printing

Fun in photography does not lie in spending vast sums of money on equipment, but in making the most of the equipment you have. I have already promised that you will be able to take extreme close-ups of insects with a box camera. If that is possible with something as basic as a box camera, what will better equipment do? The answer depends on knowing what to do, and understanding how to do it. You will be able to achieve things you may have considered 'impossible' by taking one step at a time.

In this chapter I am going to help you make better and more permanent prints than those you made in the sun in Chapter 2. If you are impatient to take some more photographs, and are content with your daylight prints for the time being, move on to the next chapter. You can read this chapter later.

You probably have several sheets of your photographic printing paper left. Keep them well wrapped in their original pack. For more permanent prints you *have* to work in a dark-room.

What is photographic paper?

It will be useful if you understand what photographic printing paper consists of. There are certain silver salts, called silver halides, which darken on exposure to light. You've already been using that fact to make prints in the sun. However, even if the exposure to the light has been brief, the silver halides will have been affected. There will be no noticeable effect on the printing paper yet, but the silver *will* darken in a photographic developer. As in your sunlight prints, the amount of darkening will depend on the tone at any particular point on the negative. You stop the action by using a photographic **fixer**, which is a chemical solution for removing the unaffected silver halides. This makes the print permanent.

Safelights

Photographic printing paper is specially designed *not* to be sensitive to red light. Most makes are not even sensitive to yellow, orange, or brown light. That means that you can open a packet of paper in a 'safe' coloured light and not spoil it. This is the origin of the name **safelight**. The instructions with your paper will tell you the recommended safelight colour. If in doubt, use red. Red is safe for all makes of bromide (enlarging) paper.

Safelights are quite expensive to buy. Early photographers used candles behind coloured glass. You can use a cycle lamp either with a red glass, or red or brown cellophane over clear glass. Only use yellow if it is a proper photographic safelight filter. You can easily check if your safelight is 'safe', and I shall be explaining how to do that in a moment.

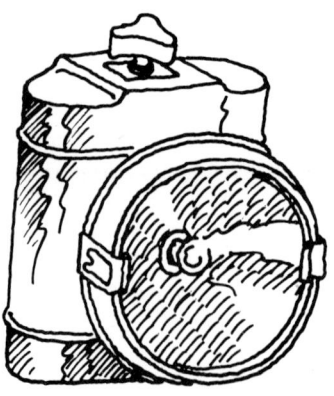

Cycle lamp with red glass

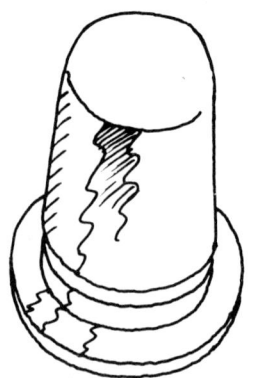

'Proper' safelight

Black-outs!

The room where you are going to do your printing must be properly blacked-out. If you make a wooden frame and cover it with black polythene, you can fit this up against a window. A small window is obviously easier to cover than a large one. Running water and a sink are not essential but advisable, and most bathrooms or toilets have small windows as well as running water. Whatever room you choose, measure the window carefully. Nail and glue your wooden frame together, and cover it with black polythene sheeting. You may need to make clips to hold this frame tightly against the window.

Turn out the light and stand in the centre of the room. If you have a cupboard under the stairs that is large enough to work in, you may not need to make any special black-out frame. Wherever you are, watch for patches of light. The door can easily be covered with a blanket if that is a problem.

If you are having real difficulty in finding a suitable room then remember you can do all your printing after dark. Just drawing the curtains or hanging a blanket across the window may be sufficient. How dark does the room need to be? It will be almost impossible to black out every single chink of light. After a couple of minutes you will probably start to see more light as your eyes adjust to the darkness. If you can count all your fingers (with the safelight off!) by looking down at them, try some extra black-out. For the purpose of printing, though, a dark-room does not have to be as black as a coal mine. If you process your films later on, you will then have to achieve almost total blackness. Photographic printing paper is not nearly as sensitive to light as camera film. With films, you will not even be able to use a safelight!

Types of paper

When you bought your first packet of paper, you probably bought a **normal** or **contrasty** grade. What different sorts of printing paper are available? Nearly all the paper on the market is **bromide** or **enlarging paper**. Bromide paper is really intended for use with an enlarger, but it is quite suitable for making contact prints. I have already mentioned the different surface textures available. The type of surface has little effect on the final result, and is a matter of personal preference. Your photographic dealer should be able to show you a sample book of all the surfaces available.

The **grade** of paper is either given a number, or a name like soft, normal or contrasty. A contrasty grade paper (often called **hard**) will make a more contrasty print than a normal or soft paper. Sometimes negatives are rather on the 'soft' side – that is, lacking in a good range of tones. Contrasty (hard) paper will brighten this up. Other negatives may print with black shadows and very bright highlights. A soft paper will help the whole range of tones to appear. You will find it easier to judge the grade of paper required as you gain experience. It is more likely that your present negatives will nearly all print on a normal grade. With the number system of paper grades, this will be either 2 or 3. The exact number depends on the make of paper. Paper grades can go from Extra Soft (Grade 0) right up to Extra Hard (Grade 5). If in any doubt, buy Normal Grade (2 or 3). The photographic shop will give you advice.

If you go to your photographic shop and ask for enlarging or bromide paper, Normal grade, and whatever surface texture you prefer, you will get the right sort of printing paper for making prints in a dark-room. You may be asked if you want a **single**, **medium** or **double weight**. Double weight paper is about as thick as a picture postcard. Single weight paper is slightly thinner, but certainly not as thin as the paper in this book. Medium weight paper is usually plastic based. Plastic-based bromide papers of medium weight have generally replaced the paper bases, and are easy to use. You may not be able to choose from a great range of sizes, but you should make sure that large sheets will cut down to your negative size without too much waste.

Chemicals

You are going to need chemicals for processing this paper. Earlier on, in bright light, you let the paper change colour. Now, with a very much shorter exposure, the image is still on the paper but it is invisible. A photographic developer is required to make the image appear. This image will be the sort you see on conventional black-and-white prints. There will be shades of grey as well as black. A **universal developer** is excellent for bromide paper, and there is a wide choice of brands. I strongly recommend a brand containing Phenidone (P.Q. developer) because it will last much longer, and even a part-used solution can be kept for a day or so in another bottle. The usual alternative ingredient to Phenidone is Metol (M.Q. developer) but this will not keep for more than a few hours once mixed with water.

From the developer, your prints go into a **fixer**. Unless you are really on a tight budget, get an **acid fixer**. Don't let the word 'acid' put you off. The acid is very weak, but sufficient to stop the action of the developer very quickly. You can buy cheaper **hypo crystals** in some photographic shops and chemists, but you will need to use a **stop bath** between the developer and the fixer. A stop bath is a weak acid solution.

What to do

Let me explain how to make a print in the dark-room. The light is turned out. You check that your black-out material is properly in place. You turn on your safelight (perhaps a cycle lamp with red glass) and remove one sheet of paper from the packet. If you

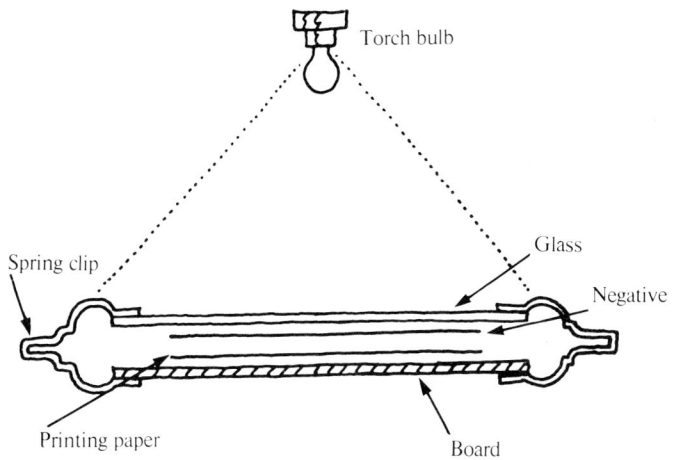

intend to buy a photographic safelight, get prices for several different makes before deciding which one to buy. You place the paper in contact with the negative and put the two under glass exactly as you did when making prints in the sun. You now shine a white light through the glass and negative.

Remove the paper, place it in the developer for about two minutes, and the picture appears. The paper then goes into the fixer for a few minutes and finally into clean water. The print is now permanent and only needs to be dried. After drying, you should have a good print to show to your friends or stick in an album. I say 'should have' because you have probably guessed that quite a few things can go wrong along the way. Let me reassure you at once. Making a print is easy. Making a *perfect* print requires quite a bit of practice.

Developer

We'll start with the developer – universal P.Q. developer for preference. You will find directions on the bottle. It will need to be mixed with water before use. Perhaps one part of developer to seven of water (1:7) or 1:10 or even 1:15. The water must be on the warm rather than the cold side. 20°C (68°F) is a standard working temperature, but it can be warmer. You will need a flat dish to pour the developer into. The paper is then soaked in the developer. Photographic dishes are specially made for the purpose, but there are several cheaper alternatives. Plastic flower pot saucers are satisfactory. Any flat plastic dish will do. Don't use household dishes unless you can keep them and use them only for photography. Glass is a suitable alternative, but not metal. Don't mix more developer than you are going to need. Screw the cap back tightly on the bottle and keep it in a dark place.

Fixer

Your developer almost certainly came in a bottle. Fixer can be bought in a bottle, which is very convenient, but it is cheaper if bought as a powder. You add it to warm water and it quickly dissolves. If you are going to mix your own from powder, use a clean plastic bottle of the type used for orange squash. Better still, get two bottles. Cut one in half just below the shoulder and use the lower part as a measure. The upper part can be used as a funnel for pouring liquids back into the bottle. Stand the bottom part of the bottle on a level surface. Using a kitchen measure and plain *water*, pour different quantities into your bottle. Mark off the different levels with waterproof tape. You have now made a measure that is suitable for all your photographic chemicals.

You can use your fixer many times before it is 'exhausted'. There will be mixing instructions with the fixer. You use it in a flat dish alongside your developer. Let it cool down if you have mixed the powder with very warm water. Some people use different coloured dishes to distinguish the fixer from the developer.

Stop bath

A stop bath is dilute acetic acid. You may not need it if you are using an acid fixer, but it will certainly do no harm. You can buy a concentrated solution and dilute it yourself, or vinegar will do the job equally well. Mix some vinegar with a lot of water as though mixing orange squash. Use a fresh solution for every printing session.

An easy test

You should now have two (or three) dishes ready for your printing paper. If the room is cold, stand the dishes in a shallow tray of luke-warm water. Otherwise, use several sheets of newspaper. These will catch any splashes. Developer will make a brown stain when it dries, and fixer a white mark. It is wise to wear an old apron when processing.

There is no special new way of handling the paper for this type of printing. Apart from working only by the safelight, you fit the paper and negative under the glass exactly as before. Daylight would be far too bright for making the exposure. So would an ordinary light bulb. You can either buy a very low power light bulb for the ceiling (about 15 watts) or use a torch bulb and battery. Don't use a mains table lamp when you have water around. A torch with a reflector will need covering with a white tissue or handkerchief to even out any bright patches from the beam.

Cut up your first sheet of printing paper into narrow strips, and you can use these to test the exposure times. They will save you paper while you are experimenting.

Are you sure your dark-room and safelight are satisfactory? It would be as well to check at this stage. If you lay one of these strips of paper on your work table and cover part of it with a coin, any 'unsafe' light will only be able to affect the uncovered part. Wait at least two minutes before placing the paper in the developer. Cover the dish with a piece of card, and leave the paper in the developer for a further two minutes. Shake the dish gently from time to time. Then move the paper to the stop bath (if you are using one) and finally into the fixer. You can now turn the main light on.

The paper should be completely white. If the paper is pale grey with a white mark for the coin, something is wrong either with your safelight or black-out.

Check it all carefully and try again. There might be a rim of white light around your red bicycle lamp, or perhaps you were holding it too close. It should be at least one metre away, and not shining directly at the paper.

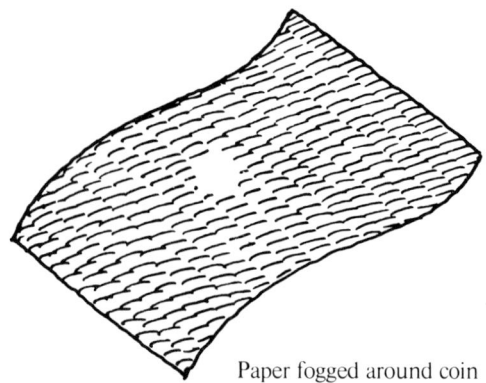

Paper fogged around coin

Exposing the print

When all is well, you can load the paper and negative under the glass as you did for making prints in the sun. (Don't forget to close the packet straight away, or you may fog the contents the next time you turn the light on!)

The exposure time will depend on the brightness of your light. You should adjust this brightness to give a correct exposure time of around ten seconds. You can only do this by trial and error. Ten seconds can be counted with reasonable accuracy and is an easy time to repeat. If the exposure time is short, an error of a second could have quite an effect on the final print. Nine seconds, eleven seconds, you will not notice much difference. Try counting with the word 'and' between numbers. One and two and three and four and ...

In the developer

You process the paper exactly as before but without the card over the dish. The time in the developer is not too critical, but should not be too short. Wait for the first part of the picture to appear. You should either be counting or using the second hand of a watch or clock. If you leave the paper in for a total of five times the time taken for the image to appear, the developing time will be long enough. In practice you need only remember to leave the paper in for a lot longer than it took for the picture to start appearing.

If the picture is going to be too dark, do not pull the prints out early to try and save a spoilt print. At least, not this time. You will need to know if the print is going to be a *bit* dark or *far too* dark. This will help you to make the necessary correction to your printing exposure time. In any case, prints look darker under the safelight than they really are.

If the picture never gets dark enough, you must increase the exposure time. You can see why I suggested using strips of paper to help find the correct time. Out of one sheet of paper you can cut several test strips. Each of your negatives will probably need a slightly different exposure time, so it is worth while running a test strip for each.

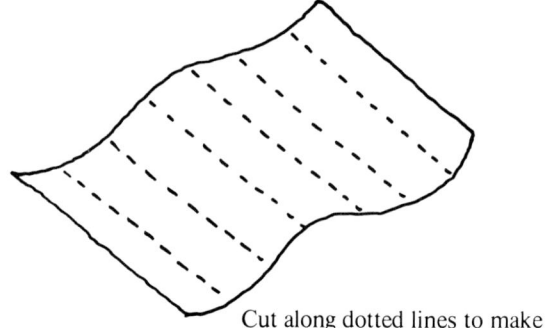

Cut along dotted lines to make test strips

The temperature of the developer is not very important as long as it is not lower than 18°C. The warmer the developer, the shorter the developing time will be. If you keep a room thermometer close to the dish, you will see if the room is too cold to keep the temperature of the developer above 18°C. When you can afford it, buy a photographic thermometer that rests in the dish. It will be especially useful if you process films.

Sometimes you will find brown or yellow stains when you examine your prints in the fixer. Using a stop bath is usually a cure for this. If that does not work, you may be leaving your prints in the developer for too long, or not getting them into the fixer fast enough. Don't examine a print when taking it from the developer to the fixer. When it is in the fixer, move it around for a few seconds. Make sure it stays under the liquid.

In the fixer

You have not finished with your prints yet. The instructions which come with the fixer will tell you how long to leave a print there before putting it to wash. It is easy to get over-concerned about fixing times and washing times. Most of these early prints of yours will soon be replaced by much better quality prints. You are unlikely to be keeping them for years to come. Five minutes in the fixer and five minutes in a couple of changes of clean water will give you a print that is sure to last for a few months.

The plastic-based printing paper has a great advantage here. The emulsion coating is very thin so the fixer can get to work very fast.

Tongs

If you don't like the idea of using your fingers for handling prints, you can buy special tongs, but be careful not to scratch the surface of the paper when it is in the developer or you will make fine black lines on the print. A few people find that their skin is affected by some photographic chemicals, but this is a very rare complaint. Tongs are a great help in keeping your hands dry. It is best to have a pair of tongs for each dish. If you are using only one pair, wash them before putting them back into the developer from the fixer. You must never get fixer or stop bath into the developer or it will stop working. Stopping the developer working is one of the objects of using fixer. The other is to remove the unaffected silver halides from the emulsion.

In the wash

You wash a print to remove the fixer, otherwise the fixer left in the paper will keep 'eating away' at the picture and it will either fade or go brown in patches. With the plastic base, the fixer only has to be washed out of the emulsion. This takes just a minute or two. Read the instructions in the packet. When you wash paper, rather than plastic-based, prints you do it mainly to wash the fixer out of the paper base, not out of the emulsion.

If you want to keep your prints for ever, then you should follow the manufacturer's fixing and washing times exactly. The easiest way to wash paper prints is to put them in an old plastic washing-up bowl, and fill it half full of slightly warm water. Every couple of minutes give the prints a gentle stir. After ten minutes, change the water. Again, keep stirring the prints every couple of minutes. Change the water three or four times more.

Some people use a wash basin and leave the plug a bit loose in the plug hole. With the tap running at a trickle, the basin will fill slowly. You must make sure that the basin has an overflow that works! When washing prints in this way you should stir them from time to time, or they will stick together in a wad.

You will probably find that the maximum recommended time in the fixer is ten minutes. There is no need to wash each paper print as soon as it has been taken out of the fixer. You can move them one by one to your washing bowl and let them float around in deep water. Then, when you have finished your printing, you can wash all the prints together. Plastic-based prints can be washed individually as soon as they are fixed. Be careful you don't drop any fixer on the carpet on your way to the washing bowl. It is a good idea to keep the washing bowl close to the fixer. Always wash and dry your hands each time you handle a wet print. If you don't, you will spoil the next piece of printing paper you touch.

Drying your prints

Your prints only need drying now. Again, the plastic-based papers will be an advantage here. They will dry without any trouble. The glossy surface (if you have chosen one) will dry to a high gloss. You just wipe off the water and leave the prints lying on a flat surface until they are dry. A clean chamois leather is excellent for wiping the water off the surface of prints.

Prints on paper are a little difficult to dry. If you leave them flat after wiping off the water, you will find that they curl up during drying. When you try to straighten them, you may crack the surface of the emulsion. It is best if they can be held flat all the time they are drying. By the way, a glossy surface on this type of paper will not dry naturally to a very shiny surface. The only satisfactory way to get this gloss is to use a special heated dryer with a highly polished metal surface.

Photographic blotting paper can be used to hold the print flat during drying. It is best to wipe the excess water from the print before putting it between the blotting paper. Ordinary blotting paper will probably fall to pieces, and fibres will stick to the surface of the print.

Extra help

I strongly recommend the plastic-based printing paper. It is quick and easy to process. It washes in a short time, and dries completely flat by itself. Whereas a paper print can take all night to dry, a plastic-based print is dry in a matter of minutes. But it is possible to buy the older type of printing paper very cheaply indeed from some sources, and it may be worth while accepting the disadvantages. You can buy a special heated dryer for these prints. Look in the photographic magazines for advertisements of these dryers or ask your dealer.

Safety

Now just a word about safety. These black-and-white chemicals are safe enough to use around the home, but *do* mark your bottles clearly. Put them high up out of the reach of young children and remove any other label from the bottle. Photographic chemicals can go strange colours when they have been used, and might be mistaken for whatever the bottle contained originally! In any case, you will need to be able to distinguish your developer from your fixer next time you do some printing.

If the worst comes to the worst and you end up with badly curled *paper* prints, you can straighten them by pulling them gently but firmly from between the pages of a book. Bend the print back as you pull so that the pulling *and* the bending straighten the print. It is better to do this gradually rather than attempt to do it in one go. Practise with an old print because you will almost certainly crease your first one.

Some of your negatives will be easier to print than others. The very thin ones (nearly clear film because of underexposure) will not give rich dark tones. A more contrasty grade of paper will be some help, but these underexposed negatives can never be printed very satisfactorily. The detail in the shadow areas is simply not there on the negative. In any case, you are probably getting fed up with printing the same set of negatives and would like some new ones. It is now time to take some more.

7 Closer and closer

When you tried photographing the toys or models on your first film in Chapter 1, you may have found that very little – or none – of the picture was in focus. You have already seen that simple cameras without focusing adjustment will not work very close to the subject. These cameras are meant to be simple to use so there are no settings to forget about. If the weather is good, and the subject far enough away, you just press the shutter and can be sure of an acceptable result.

With a simple camera the snag comes when you want to take a photograph of something small. If you keep to the recommended distance, the object will be far too small in the photograph. If you come close, it will be badly out of focus.

Close-up lenses

A close-up lens is the answer. A **close-up lens** is a magnifying glass specially made to work with a camera lens and allow your camera to come very much closer. Close-up lenses come in three standard 'strengths'. No. 1 will focus the camera at about 800 mm, No. 2 at about 450 mm, and No. 3 perhaps as close as 250 mm.

A close-up lens looks like a circle of flat glass. However, if you look through it you will see that it magnifies very slightly. You can buy close-up lenses in metal mounts to fit most cameras. Take your camera to the shop to get one the right size for your lens. It is cheaper to buy just the glass and make your own holder out of cardboard, or find some other way of attaching it to the front of your lens. You may be able to buy an 'odd' size from a bargain box and find a way of making it fit, perhaps using sticky tape.

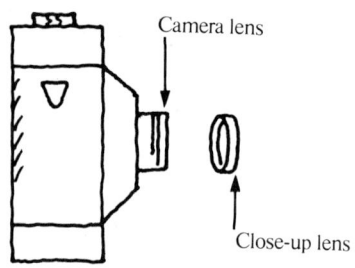

A No. 1 lens is the least powerful. It will probably be the best one for focusing on toys and models. You will want some of the background or scenery in the photograph, so you won't want to come very close.

If your camera has no focusing adjustment, you will find that a No. 1 close-up lens will bring your camera to within about 800 mm of the main point of focus. When you are using close-up lenses you measure from the front of the lens. Without one, you measure *from the back of the camera*. It is very important to get this right. There will be a focusing table with the close-up lens which will help you set up your camera. If your camera has a range of focus settings, then each setting will give you a new distance with the close-up lens. The table here gives some examples. Cameras that have no focusing adjustment are usually focused somewhere between four and five metres. (Their small aperture gives the depth of field from 2 metres to infinity (far distance) in normal use.)

Here is the sort of guide you will get with your lens. I say 'guide' because you may find that with your particular camera and close-up lens combination, the focusing is very slightly different.

No. 1 lens

Camera focused on infinity is now focused one metre from *lens*.

Camera focused on four metres is now focused 800 mm from *lens*.

Camera focused on one metre is now focused 500 mm from *lens*.

No. 2 lens

Camera focused on infinity is now focused 500 mm from *lens*.

Camera focused on four metres is now focused 445 mm from *lens*.

Camera focused on one metre is now focused 335 mm from *lens*.

No. 3 lens

Camera focused on infinity is now focused 330 mm from *lens*.

Camera focused on four metres is now focused 305 mm from *lens*.

Camera focused on one metre is now focused 250 mm from *lens*.

Note

A camera without any adjustment for the focusing is likely to be fixed permanently on four metres.

Taking the picture (*Photo No. 6*)

If your camera has aperture settings, close the aperture down as far as you can. (This is called **stopping** the lens down.) There are two advantages. The smaller the aperture – the greater the depth of field. To make your models look realistic, you will need a large depth of field (have plenty in focus). The second advantage is overall lens performance. A camera lens with a close-up attachment will work better (make sharper pictures) if you are using only the centre of the lens.

You will need to mount the camera firmly. A camera tripod is worth buying if your camera has a threaded hole for one in the base. If in doubt, ask your photographic dealer. When you are in his shop, don't be tempted to buy a new camera! You still have more to learn about your present model. When you see the results, they may turn out to be better than you think!

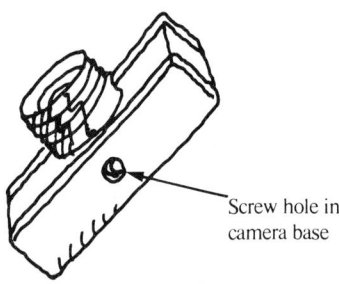
Screw hole in camera base

An alternative to a tripod is to make a cloth bag, about 200 mm by 300 mm. Half fill this with rice or dried peas and seal the end. You can place this bag on a chair back or anything firm, and rest the camera on it. The contents hold the camera steady.

Your subject will be stationary. You have all the time in the world. Using the focusing table, check your distance from the front of the lens to the main part of the picture. Stop the lens right down. This applies even if you have a camera that focuses close enough without needing a close-up lens – except here you measure from the *back* (or film plane) of the camera. You need the maximum depth of field. Work out the shutter speed to suit this small aperture.

35 mm

What your viewfinder sees

35 mm

What your lens sees. Be warned!

Hold it! How much is in the picture? Is your viewfinder still accurate? If you have a single-lens reflex or a monorail camera, you will see the picture made by the lens on the focusing screen. If you have a viewfinder on top of the camera, it is seeing slightly higher than the camera lens. The amount seen left to right is fairly accurate, but the viewfinder will see too much sky and not enough ground – or whatever scenery you are photographing.

35 mm

A set-up like this is easy in the garden. A sheet of paper, some models and you have the basic components. Sprinkle sand to hide the models' stands, use small weeds for bushes and trees, use ... well, let *your* imagination take over now

Using a tripod

Now, if you are buying a tripod, get one with a **centre column**. With a centre column you can get over this problem. The problem, caused by the different positions of lens and viewfinder, is known as **parallax**. You measure the distance between the centre of the lens and the centre of the viewfinder. You mark this distance off on the tripod centre column. (You *could* do it with a pile of books instead of a tripod.) You set the camera up with the lens rather too low, but with the viewfinder at the right height. When you are satisfied with the scene, you *raise* the camera by the distance you have just measured, and the *lens* is now where your *viewfinder* was. The picture you take will be the picture you saw. A twin-lens reflex becomes a sort of single-lens reflex, but slower to operate.

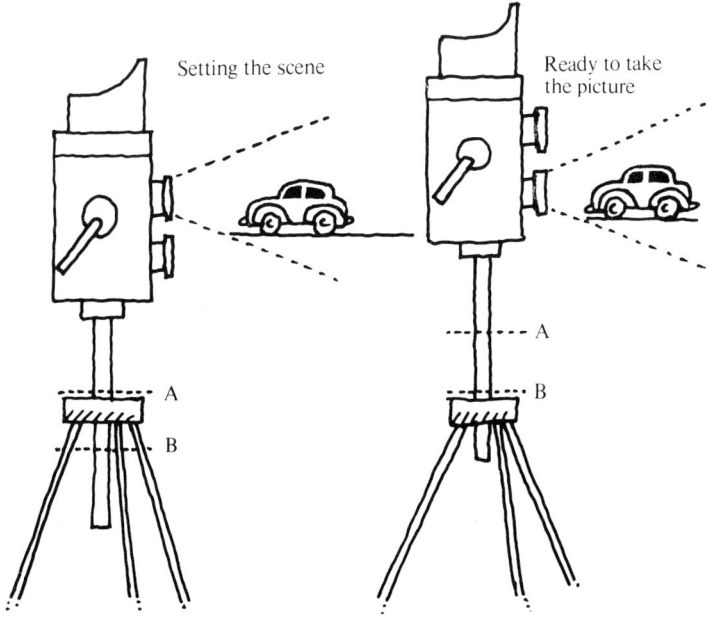

Marks 'A' and 'B' are the same distance apart as the two camera lenses

Viewfinders

Some viewfinders are to one side of the camera. To adjust the camera to allow for this, you would have to move the camera not only up, but sideways. Very difficult. A better way is to use the wire frame from page 54. Take it off the camera. You can look through this and then put the camera in the same place. Even without a frame you can look along the centre line of the lens, first on top of the camera, and then at the side. The viewfinder will tell you roughly how much is in the picture, and the two sightings will show you what part of the scene is going to be the centre.

There *must* be a better way, and there is. When you come to work on insects and flowers, we are moving even closer. Try and have your camera empty now, because it is possible to open the camera back and check the focusing with most cameras. With a No. 1 close-up lens it isn't really necessary. I am taking you through this, one step at a time.

Coming closer

I mentioned earlier that as well as No. 1, you can buy No. 2 and No. 3 close-up lenses. Which one is best? For photography of models and similar layouts you will find the working distance of a No. 1 lens about right. No. 2 brings you closer, but you may well find that the next step is straight from a No. 1 to a No. 3.

A close-up (**supplementary**) lens more powerful than No. 3 will be difficult to use with an ordinary camera. You will be working 250–300 mm from the lens of the camera to the subject with a No. 3 lens. Depth of field will be *very* limited, even at small apertures. The focusing guide with the close-up lens will probably not be very accurate, but your focusing *must* be spot on.

'B' and 'T'

You can only do this next experiment if your camera is empty. Also, you must be able to keep your shutter open. Some cameras have no shutter settings that allow this to happen. See if you have either a 'B' or a 'T' marked on the camera, or perhaps both. 'B' allows you to hold the shutter open. When you release the button, the shutter closes. 'B' stands for **Bulb**. Early photographers held their shutters open for long exposures by squeezing a rubber air bulb connected to the shutter by a tube. 'T' stands for **Time.** When you press the shutter, it will open. Even if you let go, the shutter remains open. Only when you press the button again (or move the lever back), does the shutter close. This saves the photographer getting tired hands on very long exposures!

Using a 'B' setting, you have to keep pressing the shutter release to hold the shutter open. You can buy a cable release with a lock on it which will hold the shutter open by itself. You can also get cable releases without this lock, but these are only suitable for cameras with a 'T' setting if you want them to hold the shutter open. If you have neither a 'B' nor a 'T' setting, you will have to use the tables with your close-up lens, and make adjustments to the camera distance after you have seen your first results.

Ground glass

Those of you with 'B' or 'T' shutters will need a piece of ground glass or the equivalent. Ground glass is an ordinary piece of thin clear glass that has been roughened so much on one side that it appears cloudy.

Open the back of your camera. Measure the width of the opening where the film runs, and get a piece of glass to bridge the gap, just wide enough to rest along the edges where the film runs. First cut a piece of thick card to your measurements and try it in the camera back. Does it rest flat against the opening? Is it in the

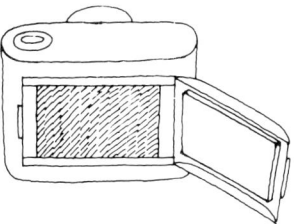

same place as the film would be? Only when you are sure it is the right size do you buy your piece of glass.

A photographic dealer may be able to get you a piece of ground glass but it is unlikely. It is easier to go to a shop that sells glass and get them to cut you a piece of thin clear glass to size. Ask for the edges to be smoothed. This will cost only a little more and makes it much safer to handle.

Your next stop will be a hardware or motor accessory shop. You need a sheet of wet-and-dry paper. Ask for Grade 180 (or similar). It looks like dark sandpaper. You use it in the same way as sandpaper, but with water. When you get home, lay a few sheets of newspaper on a very flat surface. Fold the wet-and-dry paper to make a pad. Dip the pad in water and when it is wet, start rubbing the glass. Keep rubbing right to the corners, and keep wetting the pad. After a while re-fold the paper, and use a fresh part.

Nothing will seem to be happening. All ground glass looks clear when it is wet. Rinse your sheet of glass in clean water and dry it gently with a towel. When it is really dry you will see that the glass is no longer completely clear. It is getting slightly cloudy. You still have a long way to go!

If you cannot get wet-and-dry paper, you can use a scouring powder such as Vim on a damp cloth. Don't make the cloth too wet, and use plenty of powder.

If you think both these methods sound like too much hard work, you can use greaseproof paper as a substitute for ground glass. You will have to stick the greaseproof paper on to a piece of glass, and you may need to experiment with the adhesive before it sticks flat enough.

A focusing screen

When the ground glass is ready, you have made a **focusing screen**. Open the lens aperture to its widest setting and place the ground glass in the back of the camera. The rough side goes *towards* the lens. Looking through the shiny side, you will now see an upside down picture of the view in front of you. Look on the *surface*

of the screen, and not right through it at the lens. You can alter the focusing on the lens and see how it affects the image. All lenses turn the picture upside down.

Now fit your close-up lens. I am going to assume that you have bought a No. 3 lens. It is much easier to see in the focusing screen if you look at something bright, especially if you have a simple camera with a small aperture lens. Look at the edge of a window frame, looking from inside the room out into the daylight. If your windows are very clean, you could stick some small scraps of newspaper on the glass. There is no need to use adhesive, they will stick by themselves if you wet them.

Accurate focusing

Now look through the focusing screen again. Move the camera backwards and forwards until you are sure you have found the best point of focus. If you use a table, you can rest the camera and move it backwards and forwards a few millimetres at a time. Also, you can look at the screen through a magnifying glass to be absolutely sure of the sharpest point of focus. You need to know how far the camera is from the window.

You must now measure this distance *very* accurately. Try and get it to the nearest millimetre. It is worth trying this several times, and seeing if you come up with the same measurement every time. Write down the final measurement in case you forget it. The camera must be absolutely square on to the window.

Before you move the camera, you have another measurement to make. Using a wax crayon or pieces of wet paper, mark on the window the left and right hand edges of the limits of the picture which you see on the ground glass. Also the top and bottom. This will either be a rectangle or a square.

A close-up frame

You are going to make a frame to these measurements. You can use wire or thin sticks. Balsa wood is easy to work with. Make a rectangle or square the same size as your measurements from the window. This frame will tell you how much is going to be in your picture.

The frame is going to be fixed to your camera, exactly the same distance from the camera as the window was from the camera. You can see why it is important to get these measurements correct. If you deliberately make the sticks that join the frame to the camera too long, you can lower the camera towards the frame. When it is the right distance away, run sticky tape around the camera body and the sticks. You can then cut the sticks to their correct length.

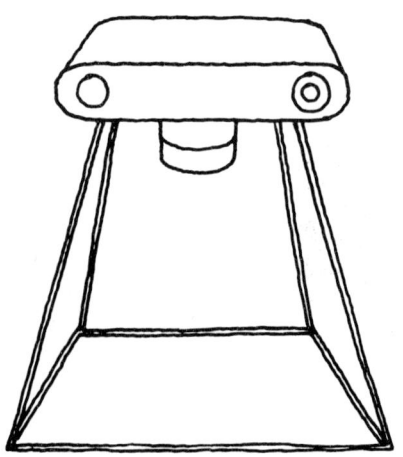

A

35 mm

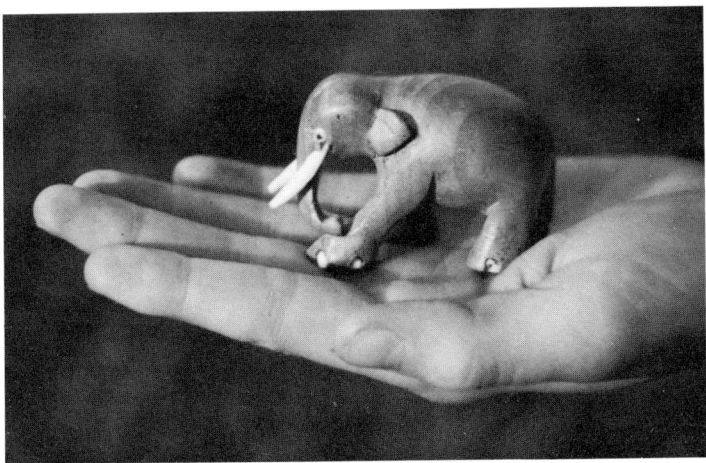

Box

B

Instead of the elephant, I could have used a pet mouse or a hamster. Here, the grass is out of focus because it is far away. Turn back to page 80 and you will see the difference between using the ground and the sky as the background

You may be able to think of a better way to fit the frame to your own particular model. It should be easy to take the frame off and replace it as often as you need for close-up work.

I'm sure you've realized how the frame is going to be used! You no longer need to measure the distance between the camera and the subject. You do not even need your viewfinder. Fit the No. 3 close-up lens, load the camera, and go out into the garden. Perhaps it would be wise to check the focusing first, using the marks on the window. Open the lens aperture wide for this test.

Set your lens to its smallest aperture (highest f number) if the frame is made correctly and, using your exposure guide, set the shutter speed to suit the aperture. You are now ready to use it. If you place the frame around the subject to be photographed in close-up, the distance setting will be exactly right. The frame will tell you what is going to be in the picture. It is not always possible to get fast-moving insects to stay still for you, so try a pet mouse or hamster. Don't let its head come closer than the frame. It is the head that you want sharply in focus. Imagine the frame marks the edges of a solid sheet. This imaginary 'sheet' must just touch the head of the mouse in order for the head to be in focus.

Flowers, model soldiers, leaves, stamp collections, other photographs, insects and any small object can be photographed easily using the frame. If an edge of the frame shows on the negative, you can trim it off on the print. When you have used this system with success you *can* try an even more powerful close-up lens. However, the depth of field (amount in focus) will be *very* limited. You can use two lenses together, if you like, to increase their strength.

If you have a camera without a 'B' or 'T' shutter setting, or you don't want to make a frame, then use a stick, cut to the right length, held underneath the camera. Just before you take the picture, let the stick drop. This will help you keep to the right distance. If the focusing is wrong, change the distance slightly for the next film.

Many close-up lenses do not give very sharp results from edge to edge of the picture. The smaller the lens aperture used, the sharper the results are going to be. You may find that when copying a page of a book only the centre is sharp. These next three pictures were taken with three very different cameras. There seems to be little difference between the results. If, instead of a grasshopper, I had copied part of a page of a newspaper, there would be an obvious difference between the three cameras. But I kept the grasshopper in the centre of the picture. The plant does not need to be sharply in focus. In the third photograph it is difficult to tell if the plant is blurred because of the cheap lens on the box camera, or if it is out of focus. If you have doubts about the performance of your camera lens, keep the main point of interest towards the centre.

When you have made this close-up frame, you will be amazed how easy it is to take close-ups. You can hold the camera in your hand just as easily as you can when taking more distant pictures. Don't forget, though, to make sure you have fitted the close-up lens as well as the frame to your camera!

S.L.R.

Folding

Box

Folding

Just so that you can see that it was not an enormous grasshopper!

8 Photography indoors

Indoor photography presents a few problems we have not met previously, but if you have been reasonably successful with your photographs so far, you will find indoor photography very straightforward.

There are three main ways of taking photographs indoors. Do you remember how you can alter the shutter speed to govern the amount of light reaching the film? When the light is bright you can use a high shutter speed, but in dull weather you need a slow shutter speed, unless you have a wide aperture lens.

Even a dull day out of doors is *much* brighter than ordinary room lighting, although you might not think so. If you need a slow shutter speed out of doors on a dull day, you will need a very long time indeed indoors – perhaps as long as five seconds at f/16! This is the first and simplest way of taking pictures indoors. Use the ordinary electric light and a long exposure.

If your camera has 'B' or 'T' shutter settings you will find it easy to open and close the shutter, giving an exposure time of one second or longer. Others of you may have shutters with speed settings you can alter from 1/500 down to one second. At wider apertures, one second may be adequate. If you have only one fixed shutter speed you will not be able to take photographs in this way, but there are alternatives.

One alternative is to increase the amount of light. If you use extra lighting, you can light the room as brightly as you like. Mind you, the amount of light you are accustomed to out of doors on a sunny day would seem unbearable indoors. If you want to get really bright lighting photographic shops will sell you **photo-**

graphic flood lights, but these are expensive. If you use a high speed film and a fairly wide aperture you will not need much extra in the way of room lighting.

The third way of taking photographs indoors is to use flash. All modern cameras (other than some cheap plastic models) have what is called **flash synchronization**. As the shutter opens for the exposure, two internal metal contacts close. If you have a flash gun fitted to the camera, these contacts work as a switch, firing the flash. The picture is taken by the light from the flash, and the shutter then closes. These contacts are fixed so that they fire the flash when the shutter is fully open. Cameras that take flash-cubes may fire the flash by having a lever that strikes the cube. In any case, the flash fires when the shutter is open.

Long exposure times

Each indoor photography method has its advantages and disadvantages. Starting with ordinary lighting and long exposures,

Box

Four seconds exposure in the kitchen. Some daylight from window. Camera resting on kitchen unit. Electric light helps to fill in the shadows

the chief advantage is cost. If you can fix the camera somewhere steady, and make sure any people in the picture stand absolutely still, the results will be excellent. You can choose a small aperture and give a very long exposure time if necessary.

There are, of course, disadvantages. It may not always be convenient to ask people to stand still. Also, unless you have a tripod, there may not be anywhere suitable to rest the camera. (But see page 98.)

The problem is knowing the exposure. Up to now, I have recommended that you use the exposure guide which was packed with the film. You will find nothing in the guide to help you now. If you do not own an exposure meter, you may be able to borrow one from a friend. The only other way is to experiment. I can give you a guide of about five seconds at f/16 to start you off. I have chosen f/16 because simple cameras usually have this aperture. In any case, you will probably want a large depth of field. You can shorten this time by opening the aperture. For every stop you open the aperture (set a lower f number), you must halve the exposure time.

Five seconds may not be correct for *your* film or room lighting. At least you should get some sort of result, and you can alter the time as necessary on subsequent films.

Brighter lights

If you increase the amount of light, you have far more control over the exposure time. You will not, however, improve the result unless you either want to hold the camera in your hand, or photograph people as they move around. You can use a high speed film, and if you process your own films, you can even increase this speed. A wide aperture lens will allow a faster shutter speed, but you will have to be *very* careful with your focusing. Don't forget, the wider the aperture, the less the depth of field.

So, what are photographic flood lights? You can either buy **photoflood bulbs** of 275 or 500 watts, or special lighting units of between 650 and 1000 watts. Although some photoflood bulbs will fit ordinary light sockets, they get very hot and could cause a fire. You will be able to buy a photoflood reflector with a metal socket and special heat resistant wiring. The bulbs are not expensive and even with a special reflector will not be nearly as expensive as the brighter lighting units.

Special lighting units of 650 to 1000 watts are obviously very bright. If you shine them on to people, the light will also be very hot, and the bulbs are often extremely expensive! It is worth looking into the cost of replacement bulbs whatever sort of lighting you are thinking of buying.

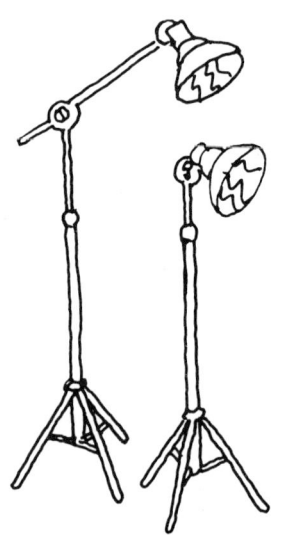 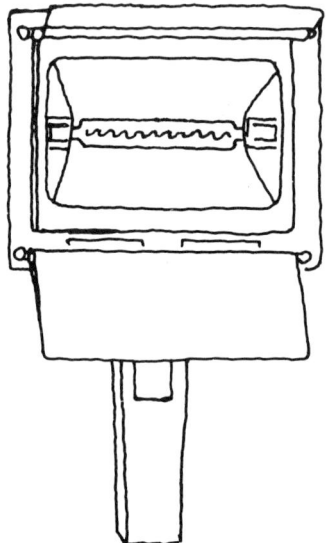

Of course, you could fit up a couple of table lamps and the main ceiling light with ordinary household 150 watt bulbs. This is the cheapest way of increasing brightness. They will not be as bright as proper photographic lighting units, but they will be useful for filling-in dark parts of a room, and can be used in ordinary light fittings (without shades).

Once again, finding the exposure is the main problem. With extra light bulbs you can try one second at f/16 using a high speed film. With photofloods perhaps 1/8 second at f/16. With two 1000 watt lighting units, perhaps 1/125 of a second, but if you can afford these units, you should be able to afford an exposure meter!

Flash

Flash! The answer to all lighting problems, or so people sometimes think. Certainly it is useful, and sometimes necessary. Most cameras can be fitted with a flash gun. Flash bulbs can only be used once, but electronic flash guns can be used for thousands of flashes.

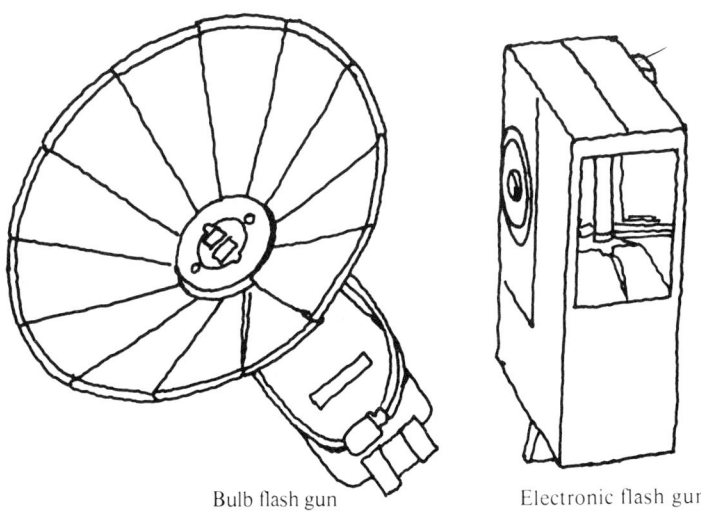

Bulb flash gun   Electronic flash gun

Using flash is expensive. If you use flash bulbs, the gun that holds them is often fairly cheap, but you pay for a new flash bulb every time you press the shutter. Electronic flash guns are more expensive to buy, but every flash is almost free. The trouble is that unless you buy an expensive electronic flash gun, you do not get a very bright flash. The brightness of a flash is given by a **guide number**. Guide numbers are very easy to use. You look at the table on the packet of bulbs or the flash gun and find the speed of film you are using in an ASA speed rating. Against this rating will be a guide number. The table will say if this is in feet or metres.

Different flash bulbs and electronic guns will have different guide numbers, but let's say that the **guide number** for your flash gun and film speed is 33. The table says that this is for measurement in metres. You get ready to take the picture and when the camera is set up, you measure the distance from the flash gun to the subject. To make it easy in this example, let's say the measurement is three metres. The *guide number* has to be *divided* by the *distance*. The *answer* is the f number to set on the aperture. The guide number in this example is 33, and the distance three metres. 33 divided by 3 equals 11. So the aperture is f/11. As easy as that.

Supposing you were at two metres? Guide number 33, divided by 2, equals 16 and a bit. That 'bit' will have no effect on the exposure, so you use f/16. Now that was a particularly easy number. A guide number of 39 would have been more difficult. At three metres you would have got thirteen and at two metres, almost twenty. That does not matter. Judge where these apertures are on your lens, and set them there. It is important to set *shutter speeds* exactly on the mark, but *apertures* can usually be set anywhere on the scale. When you know your guide number, write your own table for *all* distances in advance. You will then be able to set your apertures quickly. (Guide numbers for bulbs are usually reliable, but don't follow the guide numbers of electronic guns too exactly. Open up at least one stop more than indicated for your first film.)

Shutter speeds are important with flash. Electronic flash guns give a flash that lasts about 1/600 of a second: some even less. Flash bulbs, on the other hand, burn brightly for about 1/60 of a second. If you use a very high shutter speed with the flash bulbs, the shutter will close before the bulb has given all its light. With simple cameras use 1/30 of a second with all types of flash.

Some cameras will have two sockets into which you can plug the flash gun. The two sockets may be marked X and F. Some shutters will have a lever marked X and M. Unless your camera instruction book tells you otherwise, use the X socket or X lever position for flash bulbs and for electronic flash. Use a shutter speed of 1/30 of a second or longer. If in doubt, ask your photographic dealer. As long as you buy things from him from time to time, you can ask him for advice on how to use your camera. Don't be surprised, though, if he wants to sell you all sorts of equipment!

The main drawback with using flash is the way the subject is lit. People or things close to the camera will be very bright, whilst those at the back of the room will be too dark. Try to have the main features of the picture all at the same distance from the camera.

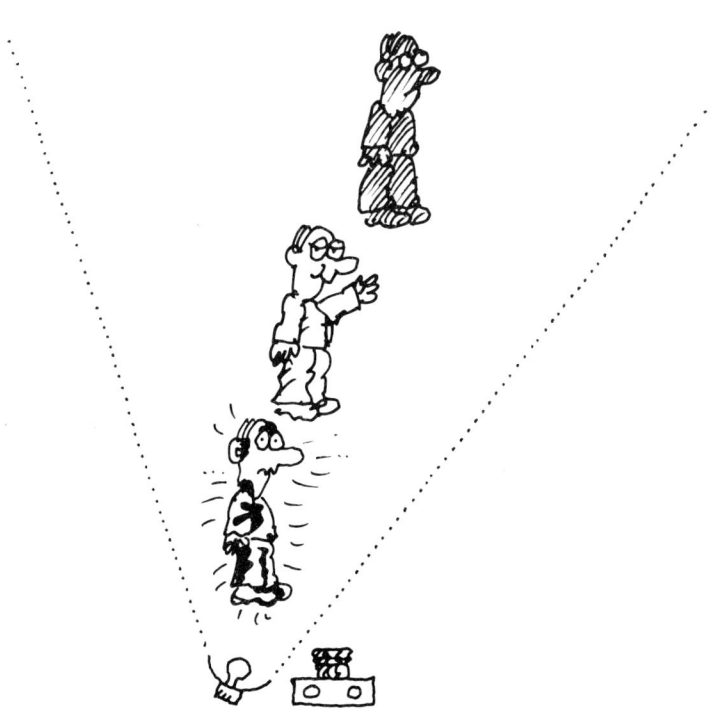

110
Cartridge

Flash can only be set to expose correctly at one distance at a time. Here the exposure is correct for the girl half-way up the stairs. Quite a good place for a photograph, though. Let's bring them closer together

110
Cartridge

To sum up

There is no 'best' way of taking pictures indoors. If you have no slow shutter speeds or 'B' or 'T' setting, you will have to use flash. I think the most satisfactory way for a beginner in photography would be to use two brighter light bulbs in the room, a tripod, a fast film, and longish exposure times. Perhaps a quarter or half a second is long enough for people to stand still without feeling awkward. The lights can stay in the same place but be adjusted beforehand to give an even brightness to all parts of the room where you are going to take photographs. The exposure can be worked out in advance, and the aperture and shutter speed set. The camera can now be moved around on the tripod, and no one will be too bright by being close to the camera. Remember, the lights are fixed to light the room evenly. You can set the focusing for each exposure, and move the camera from place to place as often as you like.

A busy professional photographer would probably use flash, and know from experience what exposure to give. It would be quicker than using available light, but I doubt if the results would be as good.

When using available light, you can judge the final effect before pressing the shutter. Nearly close your eyes and look at the scene. If any parts seem to be in heavy shadow, you must adjust the light. What you see when you nearly close your eyes will be similar to the amount of light and shade on your final print. You can, of course, do this out of doors as well. You may be surprised by how dark the shadows are. Adjust your lighting to brighten them up if possible.

126
Cartridge

Compare this with a similar photograph on page 114. Neither are particularly sharp because both were taken with very inexpensive equipment. Here, a flash-cube was used on the camera. I prefer the more natural appearance of room lighting to flash where possible

9 Processing your own films

Up to now, I have been suggesting how you can make the best use of your camera, and you have probably been taking your films along to the chemist or local photographic dealer for processing.

You may wonder how easy it would be to *process* your own films. After all, it wasn't very difficult to make contact prints using a dark-room and photographic developer.

Films differ from printing paper in two important ways. First, they are far more sensitive to light. It is no good using window black-out that has a rim of light round it. You have to find a way of making the room absolutely black, and it is easiest to wait until after dark!

The other difference is the type of light to which films and paper are sensitive. With paper you are able to use a red or orange safelight because paper is not sensitive to light of that colour. If you had used a blue glass in your safelight, though, you would have fogged the paper even if you used a low power bulb. Paper is sensitive to blue light, but films are sensitive to light of *all* colours.

You can probably see the difficulties now. Not only is film sensitive to all colours (so you can't use a safelight), but because it is so fast it will be fogged by stray light in the dark-room. But don't get too depressed! Thousands of people develop films in their own homes every day, using just the sort of room you have been using for printing. You must try and get the room as black as you can.

The dark-room

You have probably noticed that a dark-room which seems quite dark when you first turn the light off, becomes lighter after a few minutes. Your eyes are slow to adjust to the dark, but film takes no time at all to adjust! Sit in the dark-room for several minutes before deciding if you can improve on the black-out. If you are still not sure if it is black enough, develop a film and see if it gets fogged. You are unlikely to ruin the results unless you have far too much light getting in. At worst, the whole film may be slightly grey all over. To be on the safe side with your first attempt, process a film that is not very important. In any case, you would be wise to test out your processing technique on an unimportant film.

Developers

Films can be processed in print developer. (When I talk about films, I mean the ordinary black-and-white sort you buy for your camera.) It will help if you imagine you are processing a very long strip of paper. With printing paper you have a photographic emulsion coating on the paper. With a film you have a photographic emulsion coating on a clear film. Apart from that, they both need developing, fixing, washing and drying.

Without a safelight you will not know when your film has been in the developer for the right time. You have to do this by what is known as the **time and temperature** method. You take the temperature of your developer, and then you find the correct development time on a table packed with the developer. The warmer the developer, the shorter the time. Some developer instructions will only give you the time for one temperature (20°C), while others will give a range (18°C–25°C). It is well worth buying a photographic thermometer at this stage. Alternatively you can mix the developer earlier in the day and leave it in a warm room with an ordinary thermometer on the table alongside. The thermometer will give a good indication of the developer temperature, as long as the room has not been recently cooled or warmed.

To return to your film. It will not all fit in a small dish at the same time, but you can lower one end in the developer, and then as you lower the next part, raise the first part high above the dish. In this way all the film will get wet with the developer. Then you lower your first hand and raise the other. Keep doing this until the time is up. Practise doing it now, with empty hands over an imaginary dish. A roll film is about 820 mm long, and a twenty-exposure 35 mm film about one metre. A thirty-six exposure 35 mm film (1.6 metres) is too long to hold in the hands.

If you bought a universal developer for your printing paper, it should give instructions for films. You will need to know the dilution and processing time for your film. If there is a vague '$1\frac{1}{2}$–$2\frac{1}{2}$ minutes' or something similar, try using the shorter time for your first film. If you have no times or dilutions with your developer, then try mixing it 1:7 and developing for two minutes at 20°C. You would probably be wiser to buy another make of universal developer (preferably a P.Q. type) and use up the first lot for printing only. Take care to read the instructions in the shop and then you will not be caught with this bottle.

Fixer

You will almost certainly be able to use your paper fixer for films, but you will need to make a more concentrated solution. Mix another lot and label it as a *film fixer*, and change the label of your *print* fixer solution so you do not mix them up. A fixer that contains a **hardener** may make your film more resistant to scratching during washing and drying.

I think a stop bath is worth using with film, but if you have not been using one with your paper, you may not find it necessary. The chief advantage of using a stop bath is that it increases the life of the fixer. As you have probably found out already, fixer is quite expensive!

In the dark!

Now to your dark-room. Before you start, I must emphasize that film emulsion is more delicate than paper emulsion. Not only is it easier to scratch it, but you can spoil it if your processing solutions and wash water are not very close in temperature. If your dishes are rough on the edges or bottom, lay a clean polythene bag over the dish. When you pour the liquid on top, it will take up the shape of the dish and make a smooth lining.

Get a friend to stand outside the door with this book and call out the instructions, because you may forget what you are supposed to do. Remember, you will *not* be using a safelight, so your friend should be able to look at a clock and tell you when the developing time is up.

Before you turn out the light, check that all your dishes are in place, and that you will be able to tell which is which in the dark. You will ruin a film if you put it in the fixer first. Fixer removes all the undeveloped silver halides, and your film will be a complete blank. All set? Then turn out the light and sit in the dark. Don't do anything yet except look. You are looking for unwanted chinks of light, and trying to remedy them if necessary.

Even an experienced photographer should glance round the

room before starting. There may be something unexpected that is glowing or uncovered. Lock or wedge the door if you are working on your own, or hang a notice on the outside handle.

If you are using roll film, start to unwind it. A few centimetres along you will find the film rolled up with the paper. It will be the same width, but slightly stiffer. Handle this by the edges or the back, but never touch the inner face which is the emulsion. At the far end, the film will be stuck to the backing paper and you must tear it free and let the paper drop to the floor. You can, of course, hold the film between your fingers at each end.

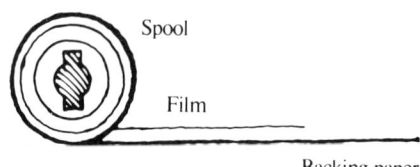

Backing paper

Cartridges have to be broken open in the middle. You need quite a bit of force to snap them. This may seem rather brutal, but they are of no further use to you. The film will be rolled up with the backing paper exactly as it is with a roll film.

35 mm film has no backing paper. You have to twist an end off the cassette. Alternatively, hit the knob end of the cassette sharply on a hard surface. With some makes of film cassette you will need a special opener, or else you can rip the cassette open. The film is stuck to the central spool with tape. Just tear or cut the film as close to the tape as you can. Don't forget that this method of developing is unsuitable for a full length thirty-six exposure film.

> You are now passing the point of no return. In an extreme emergency you can wrap the film in a paper bag and then in a thick jumper. (The bag will keep dust off the film.) Put it in the back of a drawer and do not leave a light on in the room.

Assuming that you still want to go ahead, hold one end of the film in your left hand, and unroll the film until you are holding the other end in your right hand. If the film feels very stiff and curly you can soak it briefly in plain water, but it will be too late to soak it this time unless you have a bowl of water ready. The water must be the same temperature as the developer.

However, it is unlikely you will find a film that is like this. As soon as the film is in the developer, you will find it loses any stiffness and is easy to bend. Now, place your left hand in the developer and start to raise the film in the air. The left-hand end of the film will now be wet. Lower the right hand into the dish, raising the left hand to allow only a part of the film to be in the developer at any time. This sounds more difficult than it really is.

Keep doing this until the time is up. Two minutes or so in the dark will seem a long time! Now let the developer drain back into the dish for a moment by holding the film up straight above the dish, and transfer it to the fixer (or stop bath if you are using one). Repeat the 'up-and-down' operation. Do *not* turn the light on for at least five minutes after putting the film in the fixer. You will find fixing times on the fixer packet. When you do turn the light on, if the film is a cloudy-white, turn the light off *at once*, and wait a further five minutes. If the film takes a long time to clear, the fixer is either not strong enough or it has been used too much. You should find instructions on the packet or bottle telling you the mixing concentration and the number of films that can be safely put through the solution.

In the light

If all has gone well, you will have a long strip of film, divided up into dark squares or rectangles. The dark parts are your negatives. Look at them against a light, but be careful the fixer does not run down your arm or on to the floor.

After five or six minutes in the fixer (unless the instructions say otherwise) you can put your film to wash. It is unlikely that you will be able to keep your wash water running at the same

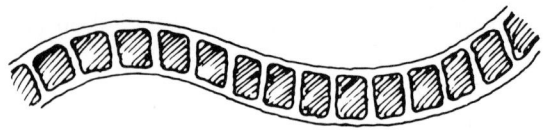

temperature as the solutions for the whole wash time, but you *must* start off with the washing water at room temperature. Let the water temperature drop gradually. The best way to wash films is to use a bowl of still water, and change the water every two minutes. After ten minutes you will find the film has been washed well enough to keep for a number of years. If you want to keep the film for ever, then half-an-hour will give full washing, but I doubt if any of your commercially processed films will have been washed for anything like this time.

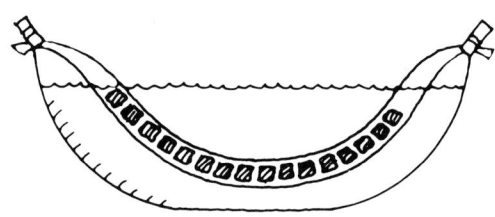

Clip the film at each end to the sides of a washing-up bowl. *Remove* the film each time you change the water, and mix some hot with the cold if necessary. You must not make the wash water too warm or you will soften the emulsion and make it even more vulnerable to scratching. A hardener in the fixer helps here.

The film is now ready for drying. A problem with drying films is getting rid of the drops of water that always seem to form on the surface. You can add just a *few* drops of washing-up liquid to the final wash water, or buy a special **photographic wetting agent**. This helps the water to run off the film when it is hung up to dry. You can buy **squeegee tongs** which will wipe the film free of excess water, or you can wipe the film gently between your fingers. Pin the film up to dry in a doorway, or from a shelf, where it will not pick up dust as it dries. Keep an eye on the film from time to time. If you see a large drop of water still on the emulsion as the rest of the film starts to dry, wipe it gently with a damp finger. If you don't do this, the film will dry darker under the drop of water.

How good?

Developing a film in a universal developer in this way should give you results very similar to those you have been getting from your photographic dealer or chemist. If the negatives you have processed yourself are too contrasty (dense blacks but pale in the shadows) you have developed the film for too long. When you print a contrasty negative, you will get black shadows and very white highlights.

The opposite effect is caused by not developing for long enough. There will not be a satisfactory range of tones. The shadows will print grey, and the highlights will not print white enough.

Compare your own negatives with those received back from an outside processor. You will soon see if there is any great difference in contrast. The final test for a correctly developed negative is to make a print. If you can print it on a normal contrast grade of paper, then you can assume it has been correctly developed. If your negative is too contrasty, use a softer grade of paper. This will help reduce the contrast. A soft (or flat) negative can be printed on a harder (more contrasty) grade of paper to brighten it up.

Although you can buy a range of contrast grades (0–5 in some makes), you will be wiser to put your developing time right for your next film. If you think your negatives are too contrasty, reduce the developing time by one quarter – and increase it if you think they are too soft (that is, lacking in contrast). Of course, you can alter the contrast by keeping to the same time and changing the temperature. Unless you know the temperature of the developer for your first film, you may find you are chasing yourself round in circles! If you have *any* reason to doubt the temperature for this 'wrong-contrast' film, keep to the same time for the next film, and check the temperature accurately.

'Special' developers

If you have ended up with negatives that are too contrasty, you may notice something interesting. The negatives will also be unexpectedly dark. So, you say to yourself, if they are darker, the film will have been made more sensitive to light. You will then decide that you could probably have given less exposure and still had a negative dense enough to print. What you seem to have done is to increase the film speed by extending the developing time.

In a way you have done this, and in a way you haven't. Film speeds are worked out in a very complicated way, and you have cheated a bit because you have ended up with a high contrast negative. So, if you bought a special developer that gave low contrast results, and increased the developing time to give normal contrast, you would then find ...

Yes. It *is* possible to change film speeds by using special types of developer. Some people may tell you that you do not alter the film speed at all, but you will find you need to use a different speed rating to get a correctly exposed negative, and that is all that matters for practical purposes.

What are these 'special' developers? There are many different types. Some will appear to increase the speed of films to two or even four times their normal rating. Others will give higher definition for big enlargements, or show the minimum amount of grain on enlargement. To get fine grain, you may *lose* film speed. You may have seen grain on big enlargements. It looks rather like a sandy texture all over the print. The faster the film, the more the grain is going to show. The grain is the particles of silver that make the picture. You won't be able to see the grain of the film on your contact prints. In fact, for contact prints you will do no better than to process your films in universal developer. It is fairly cheap, and the developing times are short enough to allow you to develop in a dish.

Developing tanks

Most developers made specially for films need long developing times. Often around fifteen minutes. To use them you will need a developing tank. Developing tanks are easy to use, but they are rather expensive when you are starting in photography. If you do buy one, you may find that these special developers give you results that are very little better than you have been getting already in a dish with universal developer, and you may perhaps wish you had spent your money on something else.

You must make up your own mind whether or not you want to buy a developing tank. You will find that a tank has one immediate advantage if you do not have a very good dark-room. You can load the film in complete darkness (perhaps a small cupboard under the stairs) and then pour the processing solutions into the tank in daylight. The lid of the tank is designed to be filled and emptied through a light-proof hole. You can load the tank late at night, and process the film the next day.

Instructions for its use will come with the tank, and as there are several different designs, I might confuse you if I tried to tell you how to use one. However, there are a few general tips that will help, so I will pass them on.

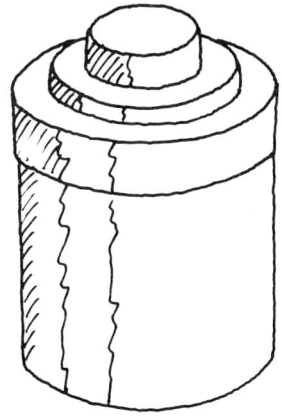
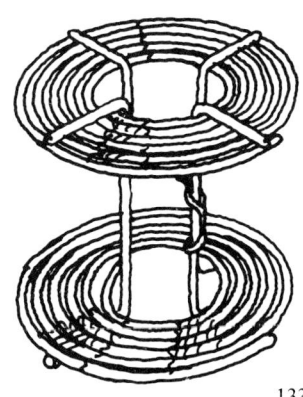

Don't expect to turn out the lights and load your first film without trouble.

1. Test the loading in daylight with an old film.
2. Still in the light, shut your eyes and have a try.
3. Test load the old film in the dark.
4. Make sure the spiral into which you load the film is *absolutely* dry.
5. Don't kink the film as you push it in or you will get dark 'kink marks' on the negatives every time you do.
6. Finally, if you just *cannot* get the film loaded in the dark and want to turn the light on, roll the film up tightly and put it in the tank. Remember to put the spiral in as well, because the spiral acts as a seal for the light. Without the spiral, you will fog your film. Try again later when you are more relaxed!

The developers that promise the most usually come as a powder. Ask advice in a well-stocked photographic shop as to which developer will be best for you and your make of film. I am tempted to say that when you have found a developer that gives you good results, *stick to it*. But then perhaps half the fun of photography is in experimenting!

As your interest and experience in photography grow, you will be in a better position to judge which developer will give you the best results for the type of photographs you are taking. Unless you can do a lot of testing, buy either a developer made by the manufacturer of your film, or else one made by an independent manufacturer. A film manufacturer who also makes developer will *not* give you the developing times for films made by a rival! It is reasonable to assume that films of similar speed rating – whatever their make – will require similar developing times, but you could get caught out. *Usually*, the slower the film speed, the shorter the developing time.

It is now up to you to practise processing your own films. You will learn a lot as you go along. You will hear a lot of nonsense talked about different developers. Within broad limits, they are all the same. Each one will give you a negative which has to be made into a print. Some will give you benefits in one direction or another, but others will simply cost you a lot of money without being anything special.

One mistake you must *not* make. Never get muddled with your developer and fixer bottles. Without doubt, fixer is the poorest developer on the market!

> A recent breakthrough in black-and-white films is an emulsion which is processed in a colour film developer. With these films you can have extremely high speed *or* very fine grain – from picture to picture – all on the same roll of film! If you want fine grain, you simply give extra exposure. (This only works on **chromogenic** films.)
>
> Although there are colour, or modified colour, developers for black-and-white chromogenic films, they can usually be processed in ordinary film developers but they must then be used at their standard speed rating and will not exhibit their almost magical qualities. Nevertheless, the results can be very satisfactory.

10 Making enlargements

If you have been taking good photographs from the earlier chapters in this book, enlarging them is the next logical step. You must not think of an enlarger as just a way of getting huge prints, but of selecting just part of the negative and making quite small prints. These prints need be no larger than your contact prints, but they will contain exactly the part of the picture you choose – and they may even be darkened or lightened in selected areas to give a really 'professional' result. Perhaps there is part of a face at the edge of a family group that does not belong to anyone you know. Perhaps you want to straighten the horizon, or move an object nearer the centre of the picture. Perhaps ...

The simplest method is to mark the area you require on your contact print and take it with the negative to your photographic dealer and order an enlargement of that particular area. This will also be the cheapest if you only require a print like this occasionally.

You could get a lot of fun out of making your own enlargements at home, but unless you are very good at building equipment, you will have to buy a photographic enlarger. And with the photographic enlarger, you will probably have to buy an enlarging lens. And together these will probably cost you more than quite a good second-hand camera. The choice, once again, is yours.

Not only is there too much wasted space, but the whole photograph is crooked. Let's select the main point of interest

Better? Something still wrong? Don't be afraid to cut out even more of the surroundings if they are distracting

Here is the final result. When you are making your own prints, you can make them any shape you like. Use strips of white card on the contact print to mask off the picture before making a final decision on what to keep and what to cut off on the enlargement. This picture is shown larger on p. 18

An enlarger

What is a photographic enlarger? If you mounted a negative in a slide projector and focused it on to the wall, you would get an enlarged picture of your negative. The further the projector was from the wall, the larger the negative would appear. If you turned off the projector lamp for a moment and pinned a piece of photographic printing paper on the wall and then switched on the enlarger for a few seconds, you would expose the paper and make a print that could be developed. The picture would appear under the developer in the same way as it did when you were making contact prints. A very long exposure time might even make the picture appear while you watched, the same way that contact prints appeared in the sun. The picture would not be of the whole negative, but only the part where you put the paper. To print the whole negative you would either have to use a large sheet of paper, or move the projector closer to the wall.

A photographic enlarger works in the same way as a slide projector, except that most enlargers are mounted vertically. They slide up and down a column, projecting the negative on to a flat board fixed below. The lens is focused by raising and lowering it on flexible light-tight bellows. Some cameras are focused in the same way.

110

12 on 120

35 mm

126

8 on 620

These are contact prints from the different film sizes used for the photographs in this book. In most cases I have selected only a part of my negatives for the final print. This improves the picture, but to do this with your negatives, you will need an enlarger – or cut down the contact prints. Some are small enough to start with!

There are two important ways in which an enlarger differs from a slide projector. First (and most important) the enlarger is light-tight. The only light that shines from the lamp goes through the negative and the lens, and that is focused on to the baseboard. The second difference is in the lens. An enlarger lens is like a camera lens. It has a range of aperture settings. You focus up at full aperture when you get the brightest picture, and then stop down before making the exposure on the printing paper. Stopping down ensures that the lens will give the sharpest print and a reasonable exposure time.

If your mattress is stuffed with money, you can go out and buy the best enlarger and the best lens. If you are not in this fortunate position, you will have to think carefully before choosing your equipment.

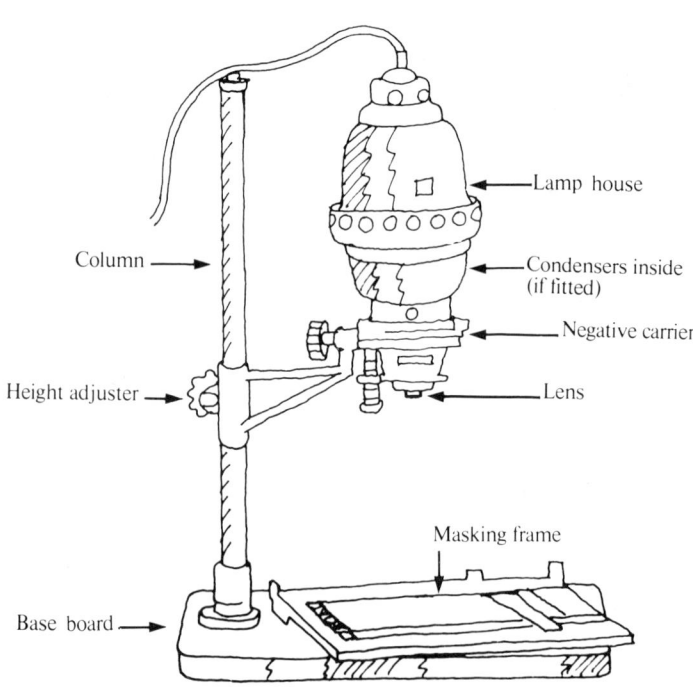

Enlarger lenses

I am going to start with the lens. Unless you are buying a second-hand enlarger outfit, you will probably have to choose a lens separately. An enlarger lens is very like a camera lens, and that may have set some of you thinking ahead of me. Most books will tell you not to use your camera lens in an enlarger, but then most books are for people who have expensive equipment. There are two reasons why you should not use a camera lens on an enlarger, but don't let either of them stop you from doing it!

One reason is lens performance. In theory a *camera* lens is corrected optically to give the best results when used in a *camera*. An *enlarger* lens is corrected optically to give the best results when used in an *enlarger*. Having said that, you may now be wondering just what these 'best' results are. I don't think they need concern you at present. You are probably so keen to get some sort of results that you are not going to look at them critically. And even if you did look critically, you might not be able to see anything wrong.

The second reason is heat. An enlarger lens can get rather warm after a time. It doesn't get anywhere near hot, but if you have just spent £300 on a camera and lens, you are going to be a little worried about the lens getting warm. If you have an old camera that looks as though it has been taken on an expedition across the Sahara Desert (*and* been trodden on by a camel!) a little bit of warmth is not going to worry it.

An enlarger will cost about twice as much as the lens. Obviously it is possible to buy a very expensive lens for a cheap enlarger, and it is equally possible to do it the other way round. But for comparable quality, the enlarger will be about twice (or maybe three times) the cost of the lens. By using your camera lens you will be able to save quite a bit of money to start with. If the lens does not come out of your camera, you can use the camera with the lens pressed against the enlarger, and the back of the camera held open wide. The shutter must be open on a 'T' or 'B' setting. Even a box camera will give moderately good results in this way. When you can afford it, buy yourself a proper enlarging lens, otherwise you can only make enlargements when you have no film in your camera. If you are using your camera lens, you may find it works better if you hold it up one way rather than the other.

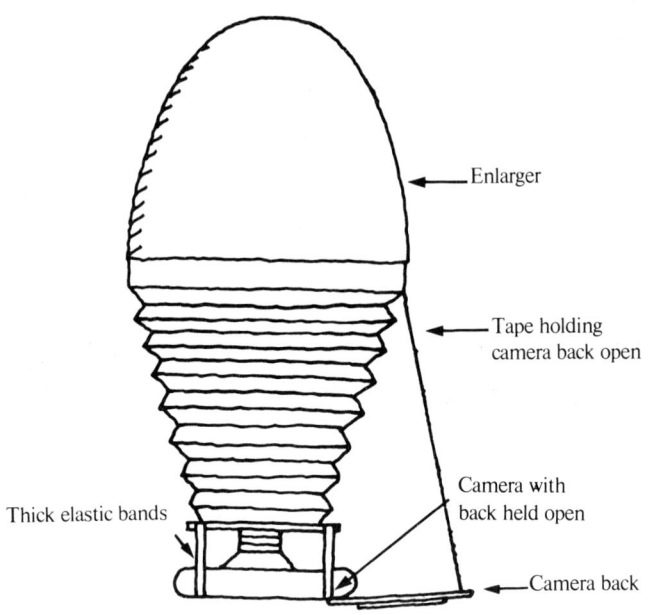

Try camera upside down and find which way round it works best

Setting it up

Now stand in front of your enlarger (or imagine you are doing so if you haven't bought one yet) and I will run briefly through the operation. The instructions with your enlarger will give fuller details, or your dealer may be able to sell you a guide to enlarging. These pages are just to help you get started – or find out what is involved before deciding whether or not you want to take the plunge.

The dark-room where you made your contact prints will be perfectly satisfactory for making enlargements, and you will use exactly the same printing paper and developer.

Now, you are standing in front of your enlarger. Plug it into the mains and switch on. Some enlargers are only fitted with two-core electric cable. Unless the instructions tell you it is not necessary, you *must* earth the metal case. An electrician will help you to do this if you do not know how. Is it earthed? If it is, you can put an old negative in the negative carrier. The negative carrier is between the lens and the lamp-house. You will find there are two flat pieces of glass to sandwich the negative between, or one piece of glass and a metal frame which holds the negative, or two metal frames the size of the negative which clamp the negative firmly in place between them.

You slide this negative carrier back into the enlarger (unless your enlarger has a different system) and you will get a picture on the baseboard. You may need to adjust the focus to see it clearly. If the picture is too large, you lower the enlarger head down the column and re-focus the lens. If you want to increase the size of the picture you raise the enlarger head.

You may not want to print the whole of your negative, but to select a small part. By experimenting you will soon find out how to adjust the height, and re-focus quickly.

Holding the paper

You may need to hold your printing paper flat while you are making the exposure. If you use plastic-based printing 'paper' it will lie flat by itself, but you will not get a white border round your prints unless you use a masking frame. A masking frame holds

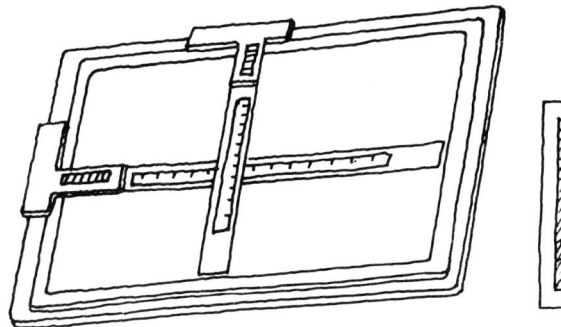

the paper flat and you adjust a moveable border to suit the size of paper. When you are setting up your negative in the enlarger, you can see the print size on the masking frame. If you are not using a masking frame, you will need a spare piece of paper for setting up.

A masking frame may seem rather expensive if you have just bought an enlarger and lens. You may be able to buy some magnetic corner pieces which hold the paper in place on a metal sheet, but again, you will not get a white border to your prints. You may not think a white border is very important, especially if you are going to mount your photographs in an album. The choice is yours – once again!

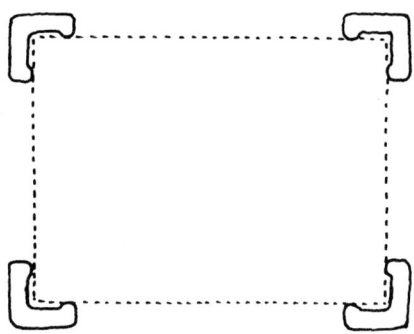

Focusing the picture

You are now standing in front of your enlarger with the negative projected on to the baseboard (or masking frame) and set to the right size. The next step is to check the focusing carefully. A **focus magnifier** is a great help. A focus magnifier looks rather like a small microscope – but costs considerably less. You place it in the centre of the masking frame and look down inside it. As you adjust the focusing on the enlarger, you will see a highly magnified part of the picture come into focus. The magnification is so high that you are focusing on the grain of the negative emulsion. Many people rely on their eyes alone for focusing, so you may not need one of these instruments, but it is a useful accessory. You must always focus the enlarger with your lens at full aperture whichever method you use to focus.

Focusing at full aperture allows you to see the image at its brightest. It also makes the picture jump sharply in and out of focus, helping you to select the sharpest focus easily. As soon as you have focused, you stop the lens down one, two or three stops. Unless you have a very dense negative, you should stop down at least two stops. Stopping down will usually improve the performance of the lens. It also increases the depth of field, so that if you made a small error in your focusing, it will not matter.

Is all well?

Some enlargers are not quite as they should be. Damage or heavy wear may throw the negative carrier or lens panel out of line. It is important for the negative carrier, lens panel (the panel where the lens is fixed) and the baseboard to be parallel.

If you stand back from your enlarger and look at the three, and then go to the side and do the same again, you will soon see if they are out of line. You may need to put a ruler under the lens and use it as a straight edge to exaggerate any error on the lens panel. If you have a very dense negative that is no further use to you, scratch lines in the emulsion with a pin. These lines

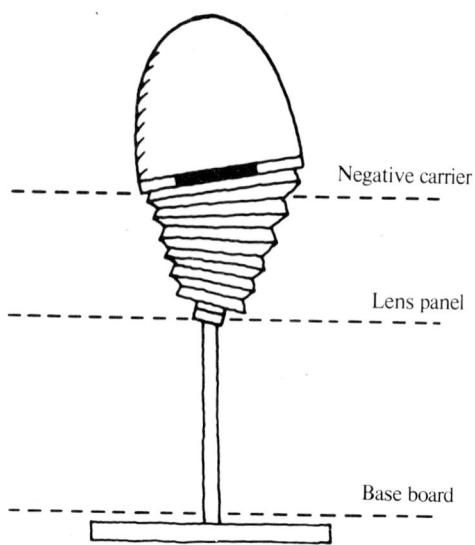

This enlarger is badly out of line! Negative carrier, lens panel and baseboard *must* be parallel.

will be easy to focus on, and will tell you if all parts of the negative are going to be in focus at the same time.

Even assuming your enlarger lens is capable of giving a sharp picture from corner to corner, it will be impossible to do it with an enlarger that is out of line. The remedy is to use card packing pieces either under the negative carrier or the lens panel to bring them parallel to the baseboard. Anything still not quite right will be helped by stopping the lens down to increase the depth of field. It is surprising how small the trouble has to be to cause focusing problems.

Test prints

I am going to assume that all is well. The negative has been carefully focused. You switch off the enlarger and place the printing paper in the masking frame (or use some other method of holding it flat). Using a whole sheet of paper may be a waste. It is more economical to cut a long narrow strip of paper from the whole sheet. You can use these **test strips** every time you print a new negative, unless you are printing a batch of negatives with identical exposures.

You cover the strip of paper with a thin book. Uncover just a part for an exposure of five seconds, and keep uncovering the strip bit by bit, giving a further five seconds each time. You might uncover it in six stages. The last part will only have been exposed for five seconds (the last five seconds), while the first part will have had six exposures of five seconds, making thirty seconds total. The other parts will have had intermediate times.

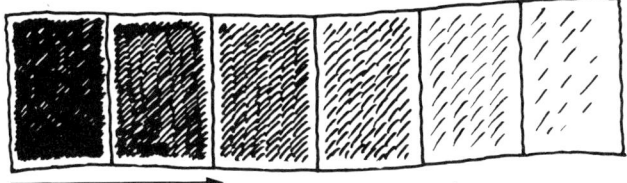

Uncover in this direction in 5-second intervals

When this strip of photographic paper has been developed, you will have a long thin section of your print, pale at one end and dark at the other. One of the six exposure times will probably be correct. This is the exposure time to use when you make your final print. As long as you have picked a suitable part of the negative, this test strip will be very useful. Of course, if you started in heavy shadow, and ended with the last part of the strip in a bright sky, you would be getting a misleading result.

An exposure time over thirty seconds is not usually to be recommended. Not many enlargers are completely light-tight. The bulb is at full brightness inside the enlarger whatever the lens aperture or negative density. There will be a small amount of stray light getting out from around the negative carrier and lamp-house. In time, this stray light will affect the paper on the baseboard. You will soon find out the maximum safe exposure time before you get a pale greyness all over your printing paper. The margins won't be affected by this if you have a masking frame, because that part of the paper is safely under the metal frame.

You can shorten the exposure time by opening the lens aperture. This will brighten the picture on the baseboard. Aim for a correct exposure time of around eight to twelve seconds. This will be a fairly easy time to count, and therefore repeat accurately. It also allows you to do something crafty – something which a professional printer will do as a matter of course. It will help you to make something special out of a very ordinary negative by altering the exposure to part of the picture.

Getting better

When you have had some success with getting the exposure right, you may find you get a bit more critical of your results. The sky may look too pale, or the ground rather too dark in one corner to be acceptable. Here is a way to lighten or darken *parts* of the picture.

Find the correct exposure time for the main part of the picture. If you want to *darken* an area, you expose the paper for this 'correct' time, and switch off. Then, without moving the paper or even touching the enlarger, you hold your hand – or a dark card – over the lens and switch on the enlarger again. You swing your hand – or card – slowly away from the lens to uncover on the printing paper the part of the picture you want to darken. You need to work out in advance which side to uncover. If you keep your hand fairly close to the lens, the edge will be so much out of focus it will not make a sharp line on the print. It is important to keep shaking your hand all the time, or you will get an artificial-looking join between the two lots of printing. Don't give too much extra printing time or you will over-do the effect.

T.L.R.

Hands too dark and face too pale. Give less exposure to the hands during enlarging. Give extra exposure to upper part of photo. Don't over-do it, or the results will be unnatural

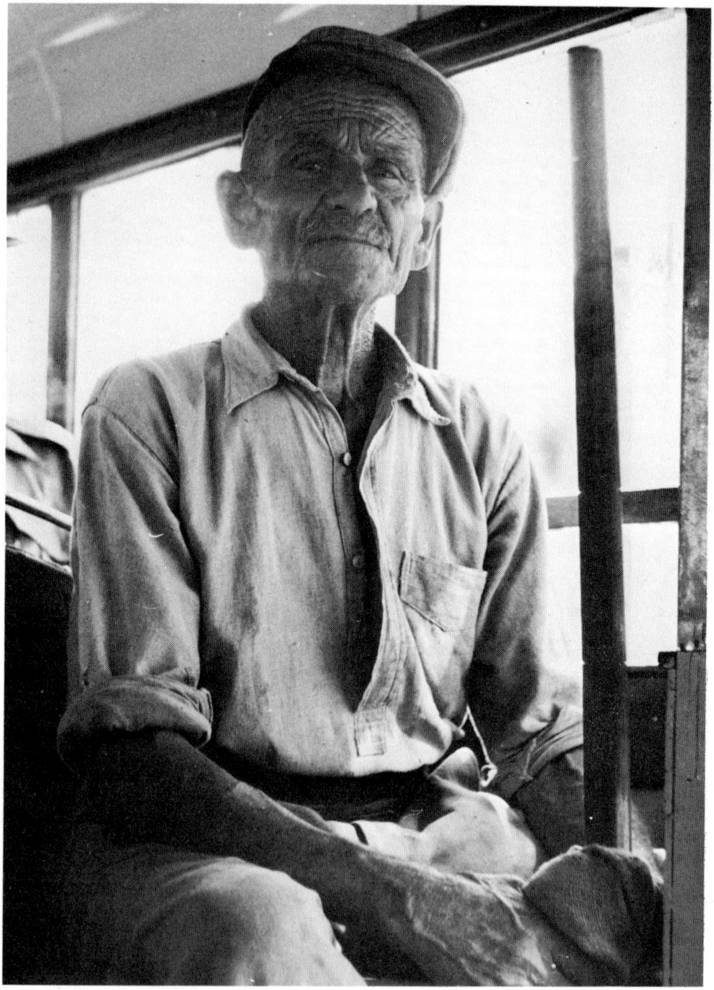

T.L.R.

A 'shaded' print. Hands lightened and face darkened

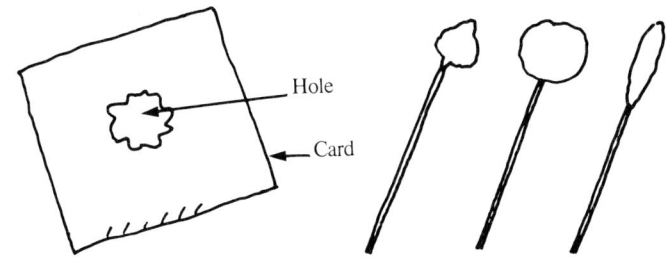

Shapes cut from card and mounted on wire

Practise doing this whole operation before you actually make a print. You make the normal exposure and then switch off. Cover the lens with your hand, switch on again, move the hand and keep shaking it as you uncover the part of the print to be darkened, and switch off. It is on occasions like this that a foot switch is a great help. Instead of reaching for a switch you press a button on the floor with your foot and work the enlarger light that way. You will find several makes of foot switch on the market. Make sure you wire them up correctly. Get help from someone who understands electrical wiring if necessary.

This effect is known as **burning-in**. If the area for burning-in is small and in the middle of the picture, you can use a card with a hole in the centre.

The other trick is **dodging** or **shading**. Find the correct exposure time for the main part of the picture, but *while* you are making this exposure, shake your hand over an area to be lightened. You will only need to do this for a very small part of the exposure. If the area is too small for your hand, you can cut out various shapes from the card, and mount them on the end of pieces of stiff wire.

This is such an easy procedure, that you will soon find it becomes a habit when printing. At the moment I don't doubt that you are thinking it is an almost impossible thing to do, but the main thing to remember is not to over-do it. Even a slight amount of burning-in or shading will improve a picture. To get absolute perfection will take a lot of practice (and a lot of paper!).

Enlarger lighting

There are three different types of lighting in an enlarger. Two of these use a bulb rather like a household light bulb. You mustn't use an ordinary bulb because it will give a 'patchy' light. An enlarger bulb is not only very bright; it has a special white coating inside the glass to give a very even light. Enlarger bulbs come as 75 watt and 150 watt. If your exposure times are too long with a 75 watt bulb, you can often fit a brighter bulb. However, it is worth checking with your dealer, because a 150 watt bulb may get too hot for your design of enlarger.

Enlargers with bulbs may have **condensers**. Condensers are huge glass lenses between the bulb and the negative which focus the light through the negative and so increase the picture brightness. Some enlargers allow you to change condensers (they come in pairs) to suit the negative size being used. This is not really necessary, and as long as you have condensers suitable for the largest negative size, you are not going to see any real difference with smaller negatives. You may need to adjust the position of the bulb in the lamp-house to obtain even illumination.

A cheaper alternative is a **diffuser**. A diffuser is a flat piece of cloudy glass. It spreads the light from the bulb over the whole negative. A diffuser will not pass as much light as a condenser, so you will have to give longer exposures or fit a brighter bulb. A diffuser has an added advantage; dust and scratches on the negative will be less likely to show up on the print. You may find your negatives print a little softer, but you can correct this by using a more contrasty grade of paper. This softness will only be between half a grade and a grade softer. It is easy to get used to this effect, and it is not to be regarded as a fault. You can either use a more contrasty grade of paper, or increase your film developing time very slightly.

The third type of enlarger illumination is an improvement (and an expensive one) on diffusers. It is called a **cathode head**. Instead of a bulb, you use a long cathode tube twisted backwards and forwards to cover the whole negative area. This tube is covered by a diffusing screen. The light from a cathode head is slightly blue in colour, and modern heads are as bright as condenser heads. They run cold and can be left on all day without harming the negative or lens.

> Some enlargers are intended for one size of negative only. Others are universal, which means that you can use the largest negative which will fit the carrier, and most of the smaller sizes. It is usual to fit an enlarging lens with the same focal length as a standard camera lens for the particular negative size. With a 35 mm negative this would be 50 mm, with $2\frac{1}{4}$ square (6 by 6) this would be 75 mm and $2\frac{1}{4}$ by $3\frac{1}{4}$ (6 by 9) about 105 mm.
>
> A lens designed for a smaller negative will not 'cover' the whole of a *larger* negative, so you will not be able to print right to the edges of the negative. The lens will pick a circle out of the centre.
>
> You can, however, use a large lens to print a *smaller* negative. The only disadvantage is that the picture can never be very big even if you raise the enlarger to the top of the column. So, buy an enlarger lens which will cover the largest negative you want to print.
>
> If you want to make *big* enlargements from small negatives you will need another lens. If not, you will find the lens with the longer focal length is 'universal', like your enlarger. Don't forget, you can sometimes use a camera lens (or even the whole camera) on your enlarger.
>
> Enlarging is a subject that can be made very complicated, but basic enlarging is really quite easy. When you feel you are ready to learn more, you can buy books (or borrow them from the library) which will go into enlarging techniques in great detail.

Most amateur enlargers take bulbs. A bulb with a diffuser is the cheapest method and is perfectly satisfactory. If you require greater brightness at a later date, you may be able to fit condensers. If you do, you will find the results slightly more contrasty, and you may therefore need to use a softer grade of paper. You will also notice that the prints show the scratches and dust on your negatives!

Lower contrast

Now for a very useful trick. If you need a softer grade of paper, but don't want to buy any more, you can soften the grade of existing paper by fogging it very slightly before making the print. It is so easy to do that you may decide to make up a jig. It will take a little bit of trial and error, but will save you keeping several grades of paper contrast in stock.

You will need a torch bulb, bulb holder and battery. If you

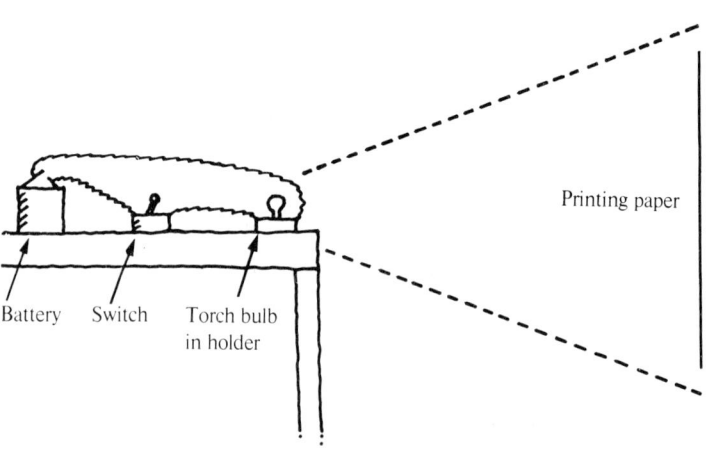

make up the jig on a board, it will be easy to use. You may have made a similar device for exposing your contact prints in the darkroom. You place the bulb and battery at one end of the room, and stand (or lean) the paper up at the other. You have to do this one sheet at a time.

Turn on the bulb for a few seconds. The exact time is found by experiment. A small amount of fogging (much too small to make the paper go grey) will drop the contrast of the paper by just one grade. When you come to make your print, you will find that the paper speed has been increased, and you will have to give less exposure time.

If you increase the time the paper is being fogged, you will drop the grade still further. Eventually you will reach a point where the paper has been fogged too much, and it will not be possible to obtain a pure white.

You *must* keep to the same distance each time, give a predetermined fogging time *exactly*, and know how much to reduce the exposure time in the enlarger to compensate for the increased sensitivity. If you are prepared to keep the necessary notes so that you can repeat the operation time after time, this is a good way of lowering the contrast of printing paper. Because of the increased sensitivity of the paper, you may need to work at a greater distance from the safelight, or you will fog the paper further during processing. There are printing papers where you change the grade by using different colour filters over the enlarger lens. Ask your dealer for details, but don't forget the cost of the filters you will need.

You must keep trying to improve your results. If you know of someone who has a second-hand enlarger for sale, ask if you can test it out. It will help you find any possible faults. The main thing to watch is that the negative carrier, lens panel and baseboard are parallel. Check that the condensers (if they are fitted) are large enough for your negatives. Check that the negative carrier will take your size of negative. Finally, check that the enlarger has an electrical safety earth before using it at home.

11 And also...

Time to get your breath back now. There are a few things I have deliberately left out of the earlier chapters. You didn't *need* to know them at the time, and to know too much too soon might have confused you. If you have found some parts of the book more difficult than others, just go back and try again. If you found too many problems perhaps you were trying too hard. After all, this sort of photography is supposed to be fun! Here, in no particular order, is some more useful information.

Exposure meters

As you have overcome many of the more obvious problems, you may still be worried by the question of correct exposure. The guide with the film is quite good, but there are always times of the day or year when it is wise to be suspicious of it. Is there a way to measure the amount of light exactly?

An exposure meter does just this. Modern ones are very accurate and reliable. The majority take a small battery which energizes the photoelectric cell. This type of meter is usually more sensitive to light than the sort with a larger cell requiring no batteries. Some, of course, are built into cameras, but this section deals mainly with separate meters.

If you are buying an exposure meter so that you can take photographs indoors, test it out in a dark corner of the shop. You should probably not be satisfied with one that is only just sensitive enough to give a reading in these surroundings.

There are two ways of taking the reading. You can point the meter at the subject and measure the light it is reflecting. This is known as a **reflected light** reading. Out of doors this method works best if you point the meter slightly down at the ground. You do not want a bright sky to 'fool' the meter. Colour slides taken on a dull day often look too dark because the meter was taking part of the exposure reading from the relatively bright sky.

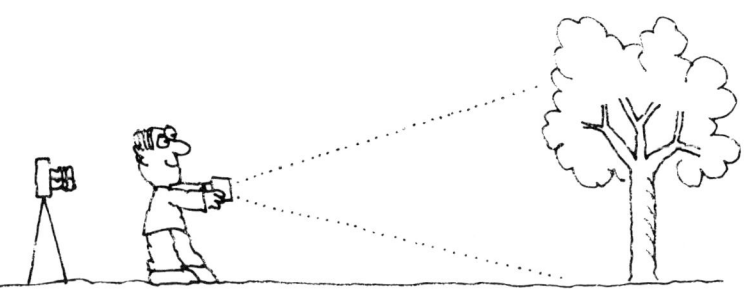

The second way of taking a reading is known as the **incident light** method. The cell at the front of the meter is covered by a white plastic cover. Not all meters will have this cover. Instead of pointing the meter at the subject, you walk into the picture and point the meter back at the *camera*. This is important. You do not point the meter at the sun or any other source (unless it happens to be behind the camera). You are now measuring the light falling on to the subject and this will give you the most accurate results for colour slides.

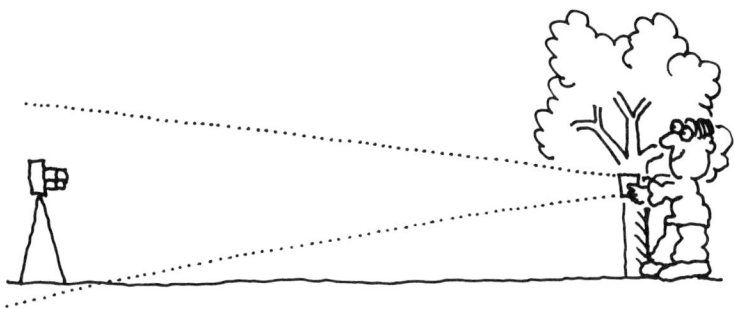

Even for black-and-white work this method has considerable advantages. The meter is much less likely to be 'fooled' by stray light. If part of the subject is in heavy shadow, take an incident light reading from inside the shadow area as well as the bright part. If detail from the shadow area is important to you, you should expose for the shadows. Otherwise, you can give an exposure somewhere in between the two readings.

There is no need always to walk into the picture to take an incident light reading. This may be obvious to everyone, but I will mention it in case it saves your legs. If you are photographing the far side of a valley you can just turn round and point the meter behind you. Just make sure that you are as much in the open as the view.

An exposure meter is not magic. You have to think carefully each time you use it. Ask yourself, 'Is there anything in the picture, or close by, that will make the meter give a misleading reading?' If there is, find a way of taking the reading so that you

---

Some of you may have cameras with exposure meters built in. There are three basic types. I am not going to attempt to explain how to work your particular one. Ask an experienced photographer or your local dealer. I will say this, though. The sort that measures the light actually passing through the lens is well worth having if you can afford to buy a camera with one fitted. (This is known as through-the-lens metering.) The second sort, built into the top of the camera is more convenient than a separate meter but not usually as sensitive in poor light. The third sort is an essential part of an automatic type of camera. It is all part of the camera's works. Some automatic cameras allow you to set your own shutter speeds and apertures instead of having to use the ones 'decided' on by the built-in meter. In these circumstances a separate exposure meter can be an advantage.

Here, it is important to expose correctly for the *shadows*. That is where you want to see the detail. The highlights will have to look after themselves!

will not be misled yourself. It is at times like this that the incident light method is a great advantage.

f numbers

Most f numbers are standard. Some cameras will have an aperture like f/3.5 marked, and perhaps other unusual numbers. It is usually easy to judge that these are about half-way between the standard f numbers shown on your exposure meter or tables. This odd number out is usually the widest aperture. An f/3.5 lens is obviously of a wider aperture than an f/4. f/1.8 is another example of this, being marginally wider than f/2. When you are wondering whether to buy one particular camera or its competitor, you might go for the camera with the wider aperture lens. Don't fall into the trap of thinking that a wider aperture lens works better than

Folding

In a situation like this, expose for the daylight on the beach. Let the shadows look after themselves. In both these photographs a light meter has to be used with considerable thought. Exposure tables with a film are satisfactory if you read off the right weather condition. An automatic camera could be badly caught out

a smaller aperture lens. It may, but it depends on the design and how well it was made. Wide aperture and lens performance are not necessarily connected.

Some old American cameras have aperture numbers that *look* like f numbers: 4, 8, 16, 32, 64. This is the Unified System, no longer used. f numbers, on the other hand, go like this: 4, 5.6, 8, 11, 16, 22, 32. The key point is 16. f/16 is the same as U.S. 16. So U.S. 8 is really f/11. U.S. 32 is f/22. If you have this system stick a new scale over the old. It is just too confusing to work out each time!

f number	4	5.6	8	11	16	22	32
Unified system	1	2	4	8	16	32	64

I only mention this because there are quite a few old models around in the second-hand and junk shops. They can give very good results, but only if you know the meanings of the apertures.

Contact printing

There are two aids to contact printing you can use. One is a small plastic contact-printing box. It is not suitable for making prints appear in daylight because it is a closed box with its own battery and bulb, but is easy to use for dark-room printing, and the light in the box can be used as a safelight, as the light shines out through a coloured plastic panel on the side of the box.

The second aid is a glass plate, hinged on a frame, under which you can print a whole film on a sheet of 203 by 254 mm (8 by 10 inch) paper. There are several versions available for different sizes of film. It is only possible to get good prints from the whole film at once if all the negatives have been exposed correctly. Otherwise you will end up with an assortment of light and dark prints. The frame is really to help the photographer to see his negatives before enlarging them. If you want contact prints to put in an album, this is not the best way to do it.

Enlarging

Unless the enlarger is mounted firmly, the column may vibrate. Tap the enlarger head and see if it goes on shaking for a long time. Some enlargers may never stop shaking if there is vibration from traffic. It is usually possible to fix a shelf bracket between the top of the enlarger column and the wall. If none of your enlargements seem very sharp, even though you have focused very carefully, vibration may be the problem.

Some negative carriers are not fitted with glass. This is an advantage if you find dust a problem. However, the negative may 'pop' slightly in the frame and alter the focusing. After you have made the print, open the lens aperture and see if the picture is still sharp on the baseboard.

Either of these hints may save you buying an expensive new enlarging lens (or even a new camera) with the disappointment of finding no improvement.

Buying paper and film

You can buy cheap paper from several firms who advertise in photographic magazines. Much of this is either ex-government or a discontinued line. You will find nothing wrong with this, but you may have to buy quite large quantities at a time. A friend might be willing to share some of this with you. If so, make sure that their share is well wrapped in several layers of black paper before taking it out of doors.

You can also buy rolls of paper in various widths. This paper is usually intended for making prints from aerial films. It is difficult to cut up into sheets unless you have a print trimmer. But it is often surprisingly cheap and worth using if you don't mind cutting it from the roll. However, this paper will almost certainly *be* paper, and not the plastic-based type, so washing and drying will take longer.

Cheap film can often be obtained from the same source. Long lengths of 35 mm film come in tins. In the dark you tape one end to the cassette spool and keep winding until the spool is full. You then cut the film and place the spool in the cassette with the tail hanging out. You can buy empty cassettes which can be reloaded several times. Don't forget to re-wrap the rest of the film and place it in the tin – before turning the lights on!

Some films and papers bought in this way will work better than others. You can only find the best by experience. But they will all work, or you can write to the mail order company and complain. Remember, though, that you get what you paid for.

Depth of field

An object that is slightly out of focus on a contact print will seem more out of focus on an enlargement, because you magnify the muzziness. This is why it is not possible to give accurate depth of field tables. The greater the enlargement, the less the depth of field. The box camera that seemed in focus at two metres may need a minimum distance of three metres if you are enlarging just part of the negative.

Other lenses

Some cameras can be fitted with wide-angle and telephoto lenses. A wide-angle lens gets more into the picture than a standard lens. A telephoto lens works a bit like a telescope. It shows just part of the standard picture, and makes that part bigger on the negative. These additional lenses come in different focal lengths. The shorter the focal length, the wider the angle of the lens (the more it gets in). The longer the focal length, the less it gets in. A powerful telephoto lens can be quite large and heavy. Strictly speaking, a telephoto lens is a lens that has been designed not to be as long as it would seem from its focal length. This keeps the size down. A long-focal-length lens that has not been designed in this way is called simply a long-focal-length lens. Most lenses with a long focal length have been designed as proper telephoto lenses, and in any case just about everyone calls all of them telephoto lenses. The fact that there is a technical difference is only useful if you are considering several different makes. True telephoto lenses will be more compact when fitted to the camera.

Long focal length and short focal length are only long or short when compared to the standard lens. 150 mm would be 'long' when fitted to a 35 mm camera where the standard lens is around 45 mm, whereas 150 mm might be the standard lens on a large bellows camera. If you give the matter some thought you will see that because of the different negative sizes, both 'standard' lenses will include the same amount of the original scene.

A zoom lens changes its focal length while still keeping the subject in focus. Especially useful on ciné cameras, many photographers find they need only have one lens (a zoom one) on their still camera. Quite expensive, though!

Colour film

More people use colour film than black-and-white film. Colour film is quite difficult to process and print at home. Apart from the processing and printing, you can use colour film for all the jobs we have been through.

There are two main types of colour film. Negative, for making colour prints, and transparency (or reversal) film for making slides. If you have a projector, you will find that making colour slides is as cheap as making your own black-and-white prints. However, there is a lot to be said for the fun of doing all the processing and printing yourself. It *is* possible to process and print colour films at home, but it is too complicated to be included in this book.

If you want to use colour film go back through the chapters on photography. With a simple camera you may only be able to use it on bright days unless you can buy a high speed colour film. Although large cameras produce beautifully detailed colour slides, it is not usually possible to put them in a projector. Cameras taking smaller film sizes are better for slides. Correct exposure is more important with colour than black-and-white film.

Filters

With colour film you should not normally use any filter on the lens unless it is an ultra violet (or haze) filter to cut out some of the purple colour you get in the shadows near water or on distant views, or a very *very* pale pinky-brown filter to 'brighten' up a dull day.

A filter is a flat piece of glass or gelatin sheet that goes over the lens. On black-and-white film, coloured filters can be used to make some of the tones more noticeable, or less noticeable if required. A yellow filter will let all the yellow colouring in the scene on to the film, but not so much of the blue. A green filter lets the green through, but again, not so much of the blue. Grass and leaves will seem lighter in tone on the print than they really are. The blue sky will appear slightly darker because not all the blue has got on to the film. By darkening the blue of the sky, white clouds will stand out more clearly. A red filter will make the sky darker still. If you are copying a book, and someone has written over a page with a red pen, you can photograph it through a red filter. The red will now come through as brightly as the white of the page, and with luck, the red writing will disappear.

The use of filters really deserves a book to itself. This book deals with the basic steps in photography, and if you are buying just one filter for black-and-white I recommend a yellow-green. This will show up the clouds and lighten the grass slightly. Older books on photography are sometimes very enthusiastic about filters, but modern films have been improved so much that for general work you will not improve your results by using filters. It is only when you want to achieve a special effect that they are worth using.

All coloured filters cut down the amount of light reaching the film, and so you must allow more exposure. There should be a table with the filter telling you the **filter factor**. A filter factor of X2 means that your ASA film speed has been cut in half. 400 ASA becomes 200 ASA and so on. A filter factor of X4 means that the ASA film speed has been divided by 4. 400 ASA becomes 100 ASA. Divide your ASA film speed by the filter factor to get your new film speed. Without the filter, of course, you expose the rest of the film at its normal speed.

A clear ultra-violet filter can be left on the camera the whole time, whether you are using colour or black-and-white film. It will protect your lens from dirt, rain and finger prints. If it gets scratched it is cheaper and easier to replace than the lens.

Instant-print cameras

Polaroid and other instant-print cameras use a special film. As soon as you have taken the picture, developing commences automatically. Within a minute or so you have a print of the picture you have just taken. As these cameras are different from the conventional camera I have not included them in this book, but if the idea appeals to you, discuss the advantages and disadvantages with your dealer. Personally I like the system, but not as a replacement for conventional cameras.

Do not confuse instant-print cameras with Instamatic cameras. Instamatic cameras (the name is a Kodak patent) do not produce the picture instantly. They take a film cartridge and *load* instantly. There is no threading of the film. You open the camera back and replace the cartridge. See page 75 for a more detailed explanation of cartridge-loading cameras.

Second-hand cameras

Good second-hand cameras bought through a dealer will have a guarantee. Most dealers will let you put a film through a camera without taking it further than the shop doorway. You can then judge from this film if the camera is a good one.

If you are taking a chance with an old camera, perhaps from a junk shop, make sure you don't pay much for it. Even a simple shutter fault can be very expensive to repair. This section is about the type of old camera that has not cost very much, but may be in need of some attention.

First of all the shutter. You must not attempt to take a shutter apart or even oil it. Many shutters will only work if there is no oil at all on some of the moving parts. The best thing to do is to check that the shutter is working before you pay for the camera. You can do this quite simply by opening the camera back and looking through the lens at the light. Press the shutter release and see if the shutter opens for a fraction of a second on the 'instantaneous' setting. If there is a range of shutter speeds, check that they get slower or faster as you alter the setting. See if the shutter stays open on the 'B' or 'T' setting. (You may need to turn the film winding knob before the shutter release can be pressed.) If the shutter works and you like the camera, buy it if the price is right. Most other faults you can put right yourself.

Focusing can be checked with a ground glass screen. Page 105 onwards will help you to do this. See if the distance scale is correct. If the camera is a folding model with bellows check that the lens stands up straight from the panel. You may need to do a bit of very gentle bending to put this right, or to tighten a couple of screws.

Most faults are going to be on these bellows cameras. If the shutter of a 35mm camera works, you can usually assume that the rest of the camera is in good order. Folding camera bellows can leak light. Replacement bellows may be expensive, but worth having fitted to some of the better models. Black plastic sticky tape, black plastic paint, or even black plastic sheeting can be used to seal the light out of the bellows. Even if you can't fold the camera again, it will make a useful camera around the home and garden. The best way to check for light leaks is to open the camera when you are back in your dark-room and shine a powerful torch inside the camera. You will soon see any cracks or holes. After all, you don't want to cover *all* the bellows with black plastic for the sake of one tiny hole!

There is one more check you can make on a camera. Look through your lens with the camera back and shutter open. If the lens looks clear then do not attempt to clean it. A few specks of dust on the lens will *not* affect your picture. Just take my word for it. Dust on the lens will not show as dust on your pictures. The dust on your pictures is caused by dust and dirt floating around inside the camera. Give it a good blow out to get rid of this problem.

Now then, you are looking through your lens. Perhaps it looks a bit cloudy. You can clean a lens with an old (but clean) cotton handkerchief. The minimum amount of cleaning please. If you have cleaned both surfaces but the cloudiness seems to be inside, the lens will have to be taken apart for cleaning. If the camera is a good one, don't do it. Take it to your dealer. It is not always possible to put a lens back together again properly. If you *do* take the lens apart, check the focusing afterwards with a ground glass screen. This could save you a wasted film.

If the cloudiness still won't come off, you are faced with a choice. A cloudy lens will never give you clear pictures, and will be absolutely terrible if you are photographing into a bright light. A good lens *must* be cleaned professionally. However, there is a last-resort home treatment you can give it and if the camera is a cheap one it is worth trying, but be prepared to say goodbye to your lens!

Gently, very gently, rub the lens with a soft cloth and silver polish. After a few rubs, wipe off the polish and examine the lens. Apply more silver polish if necessary. This sounds brutal, but I have made it work on several occasions. Please don't write to me to complain if you spoil your lens. This method is a last resort only! I have used both Silvo and Duraglit silver polish.

Most modern lenses have a blue, green or brownish coating to help cut down flare within the lens. You may see all three colours as you look down into the lens. Whatever you do don't try and get this coating off! It is very much part of the lens. Some cartridge-loading cameras have plastic lenses. These look like glass but scratch more easily.

With any camera, light can get on to the film through a badly fitting back. If you show the film and the camera to your dealer, his experience may help in tracking down the source of the

Borders fogged as well as picture area

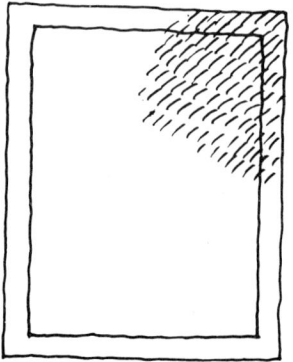

Fogged in picture area only

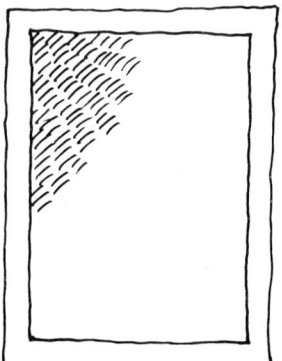

trouble. If your camera is so old you would rather not show it around, then here is a useful illustration. Two negatives, both fogged by light getting into the camera.

The negative on the left has been fogged right into the margins. Almost certainly the light was getting in through the *back* of the camera. Perhaps you have forgotten to put tape over the red window. The negative on the right has been fogged in the picture area, but not right to the edge of the film. The edge of the negative is hidden behind the metal cutout of the camera. The light must have been getting in from towards the *front* of the camera. Open the back of your camera some time and you will understand this better.

To sum up this whole matter of camera repairs. If the camera is a good one, *never* attempt to repair any of it yourself. If you can't afford to have it repaired professionally, put it away in a drawer until you can. You will never be able to get it repaired if you have had a go at it yourself. Camera mechanics will not touch equipment that has been tampered with. If the camera is not working but you feel it is not worth paying to have it repaired, have a go at it yourself rather than throw it in the bin. Apart from the shutter, most parts *can* be put right at home.

12 Putting it right

'Oh dear, what's gone wrong *this* time?' Familiar words? Don't be too hard on yourself. It will be a long time before every picture comes out exactly as you planned it. All the same, it is annoying to waste time and film. Some of your results will be spoilt by faults, and others by mistakes.

Faults are different from mistakes. Mistakes are things you make once – and then learn from! Faults are things that keep going wrong, and it's not always easy to see why. The first film you took in Chapter 1 probably had plenty of mistakes on it. I would like to think that you have been learning fast as you have gained confidence and experience by going through the chapters of this book.

Faults are a different matter, and can spoil the most carefully planned photograph. They can occur in three main places. 1. In the camera. 2. During the processing of the film, and 3. During printing. A spoilt print can be put right by making another one, but a spoilt negative – however caused – usually means the photograph has to be taken again if you want it right.

It is not always easy to distinguish between faults and mistakes, but let me give you an example of a spoilt photograph that could have been caused by either. Camera shake produces a blurred muzzy picture. If camera shake is severe, the result will be obvious. However, slight camera shake can spoil a picture just enough to make you blame the focusing or the performance of the lens. As I said, this might be caused by a mistake or a fault. If you forgot you had selected a slow shutter speed (or forgot to set the correct one) and then didn't take enough care to hold the camera steady, that would be a **mistake**. However, if the shutter was faulty, and always gave you a slow shutter speed, then you would get camera shake however carefully you held the camera. That would be a **fault**. Can you see the difference? All the previous chapters have been helping you not to make mistakes. This chapter helps you sort out faults, although you will also find some further help on mistakes.

FAULTS IN THE CAMERA

* *Camera shake*. If the shutter is faulty and always gives you an exposure time too long for the camera to be held steady, then you will find your negatives are very dark (or colour slides are very pale). However, if your negatives are correctly exposed, your camera may be a very difficult one to hold steady. See page 39 for further help here. You can carry out an easy test for camera shake. Take one picture holding the camera in your hands. Take

Folding

A good example of camera shake. The shiny button on the boy's anorak in the centre shows the direction of shake. Twigs growing in the same direction look quite sharp.

a further photograph of the same subject while resting the camera on a wall, or car roof. This will give you a standard of sharpness from your lens against which you can check other photographs. Try several different apertures (with suitable shutter speeds) to see how well your lens works.

★ *Focusing*. The previous test will also help you see if the focusing scale on the camera is correct. If it is wrong, you can re-mark it, or have the camera repaired. If you find accurate focusing a problem and there is no focusing aid on the camera, you can buy a rangefinder. Your dealer will explain more about these. Large cameras need more accurate focusing than small ones (see page 63) and the closer you come to the subject, the more accurate you have to be. More help on this on page 105.

Folding

No camera shake here. The anorak buttons are circular. Nothing is in focus. The camera focusing was set too close. If it had been set for the distance, either the tree or the far distance would be sharp.

★ *Double exposure.* If you forget to wind on between exposures, then you can expect to have a double exposure! This is two pictures on top of each other. Sometimes they are quite amusing, but they are also two wasted photographs. That counts as a mistake. Sometimes the camera wind-on mechanism is faulty, and although the lever winds on, the film stays still – or perhaps only moves part of the way. Where you can see the numbers printed on the back of the film through a red window, you should not get this fault. If your camera has a built-in device to stop you taking another picture until you have wound on, check that it is still working. (Press the shutter in the dark to avoid wasting film.)

★ *Light leak.* This section deals with light leaking into the camera, rather than into the dark-room. Page 168 will help you decide which part of the camera is leaking light. Leaving a camera in bright sun can sometimes mean light leaks into the small window where the film numbers show. This, of course, only applies to roll film cameras. Ask your dealer to help you if you can't find the source of the trouble yourself. He will have seen plenty of examples of light leak. Whatever you do, don't take important photographs until you have sorted out this problem.

★ *Long lines.* These will be very straight, and either print black or white. If they are wavy lines, they are not being made in the camera. Thin black lines are caused by a rough film roller or film guide scratching the emulsion of the film. (The emulsion is the part of the film that faces the lens.) White lines (on the print) are scratches on the back of the film. You will only scratch the back of film that has no backing paper – such as 35 mm film. Find the rough patch, use *very* fine emery paper to smooth it off, and then polish with metal polish. Be careful not to remove a large area of black paint or you may get problems from reflection. Make sure that film rollers turn easily, but be careful not to use much oil, or it will spread on to the film. The tiniest drop of fine oil on the pivots, wiped off immediately, will be more than enough. The rollers were probably designed to run dry, and may only need cleaning.

* *Specks*. Clear specks on the film that print black are caused by dust inside the camera settling on the film before a picture is taken. The dust prevents light getting to a small part of the film. If you examine the print or negative with a magnifying glass you will see the shape of the dust. Small circular spots are caused during the developing of the film – see later. Blow out the inside of the camera with a bicycle pump before loading with your next film.

An enlarged part of the sky. The black scratch got on to the emulsion in the camera. The black specks are caused by dirt in the camera. The white specks are dirt on the negative in the enlarger

FAULTS DURING FILM PROCESSING

* *Contrasty negative*. Very black parts *and* relatively pale. Perhaps easier to judge from the print if the negative is contrasty. There will be very black shadows, and white highlights. The film has been developed for too long. Perhaps the developer was too

warm. Warm developer needs a shorter developing time than a cooler one. If one or two negatives on a film are too contrasty, then the lighting on the subject was too contrasty for the film. You can reduce the developing time to overcome this, but then you will find that the other pictures are not contrasty enough! A softer grade of printing paper will help you make better prints from contrasty negatives.

* *Dense negative.* A negative that is unusually dark all over will make a reasonable print. You may find that exposure times in the enlarger are annoyingly long, but if the enlarger is light-tight you will get a print in the end. A dense negative that makes an ordinary print has been overexposed in the camera. The shutter speed was either too slow, or the aperture too wide. Perhaps you forgot to alter your settings from the previous exposure. If the print from the negative is also contrasty, then you have overdeveloped the film. (See page 131.)

* *Faint negative.* A faint negative may have been caused by not enough exposure (underexposure), or not enough time in the developer (or not having the developer warm enough – which amounts to the same thing – see page 131. Look for the shadow areas. If you can still see detail in them, then the film was underdeveloped. If they are just clear film, then the film was underexposed. An underdeveloped negative will print fairly well on a hard (contrasty) grade of paper, although you will see small scratches and other marks that don't usually appear on your prints. An underexposed negative will never print very well.

* *Flat negative.* The word 'flat' here refers to the contrast of the negative rather than its shape! (By the way, if your negative doesn't lie flat in the enlarger, you will never get a print that is sharp all over.) A flat negative lacks contrast. A print from it will have grey shadows, and grey whites. Use a more contrasty grade of printing paper, and remember to give your next film slightly longer in the developer. Light leaking into your dark-room may fog your film slightly, and give it a 'flat' look.

* *Marks*. All marks on the negatives can be avoided if you are careful enough during processing. Little kink marks are made when handling the film before processing. If you look at the surface of the film you will see that the whole film has been bent in sharply at this point. The actual bending affected the emulsion in the same way as light affects it, and makes a dark patch appear. Long, wide, wavy dark lines on a dry film are made by water running down the film when most of it was dry. Large water drops can leave their shape behind by darkening the film. Get all the water you can off the surface, inspect the film once or twice during drying, and remove these drops with a damp finger. Specks of grit or dirt stuck to a dry negative probably got on there from the wash water – or from a dusty room during drying. A *few* drops of wetting agent (or washing-up liquid) in the last lot of wash water will help the film to dry more cleanly and evenly (page 130). A cloudy brown negative has not been fixed properly. Small circular marks are caused by air bubbles sticking to the film in the developer. Let the developer stand for a bit before using it.

* *Thumb prints*. Finger prints and thumb prints will not occur if you keep your hands well washed during all stages of processing. Black prints on the negative mean that you had developer on your hands before you put the film in the developer. Clear prints on the negative mean that you had fixer on your hands either before or during developing. Take great care!

* *Wavy scratches*. These are not caused in the camera because the film runs in a straight line in there. You have scratched either the front or the back of the film at some time during the processing, washing or drying. Check for rough patches on the dish if you are not using a developing tank, and line the dish with polythene if necessary (see page 127). If you are wiping the film down with a squeegee before drying it, check that the squeegee blades are clean and smooth.

FAULTS DURING PRINTING

Before reading this list, please note: marks and other faults on a print may *also* be on the negative. Check most carefully in a good light, or you may be looking for a printing fault that is not there.

★ *A brown print.* A print that has been taken out of the developer too soon (or developed in cold developer) will not be black and white, but warm-toned. The print may be unevenly developed, and textured paper may show uneven development around the raised pattern if you examine the print very closely. The way to avoid this fault is to give less exposure during printing and to leave the paper in the developer for the recommended time at the recommended temperature.

★ *Fogged.* Stray light can make a print go pale grey all over. Although the picture is there, the whites have gone grey. Perhaps the white margins (if you have them) have this greyness in them as well. Look for light leaking into the dark-room. Your safelight may be too bright or too close to the paper. Your enlarger may not be light-tight. Keep looking!

★ *Spots.* It is so unlikely that the spots are not on the negative that you should check again. Dark spots on the print are dust in the camera getting on the negative before the picture was taken. White spots on the print are caused by specks sticking to the film during drying.

★ *Stains.* If you leave the print in the developer for too long – or the developer is very old and brown – you may get brown stains on the print. If the paper is not properly under the fixer all the time during fixing – or is not moved about enough during fixing – you may get brown or reddish-coloured stains. Make another print and be careful. If they still persist a stop bath may help (see page 87).

★ *Thumb print.* A black finger print or thumb print is caused by developer on your hands when handling the paper before processing. A white mark is caused by fixer on your hands. Make sure you have clean water and a towel for your hands during all processing.

★ *Tong marks.* If you are using plastic tongs to handle your printing paper in the developer and fixer, make sure you do not rub them across the surface of the paper when it is in the developer. If you do, you will get short fine black lines showing on the print. These will be more noticeable on textured paper surfaces.

> *Anything else?*
>
> I have not been able to list every possible fault. Blank films or paper may be caused by faulty equipment, or it may simply be that you processed the wrong film or paper! Thumbs or bits of camera case in front of the lens are easy to detect. If you have a fault that is not in this list, see if you can tell at what stage the fault is occurring: camera, developing or printing. You will then be well on the way to solving the problem by yourself.

A final word

I have before me a list of things that I could have included in this book. The problem is to know when to say 'stop'. I hope that the things I have included will have been more than enough to whet your appetites for more and more photography. If that is so, then I am pleased that you have got this far without being overwhelmed by 'facts'. I have tried to keep everything simple, helping you to find out a lot for yourself. When you started on Chapter 1, perhaps you thought I was rather unsympathetic – sending you out to make mistakes! But you learnt quickly.

Where do you go from here? Read books and magazines; join a camera club; discuss photography with anybody you feel may be able to help, and, above all, *take photographs*. Knowing how to do it counts for nothing, unless you do it, and do it well. Think very carefully before buying a new camera or any other

Never be afraid to ask people if you can take their photograph. Local shopkeepers may be very pleased to pose for you – especially if you promise them a print!

equipment. With your knowledge and a simple camera you may be able to do far better than someone starting out with an expensive model. But then if you had an expensive camera . . . Ah well, you can always dream. Meanwhile, enjoy the equipment you can afford. Perhaps these will be your most enjoyable moments of photography.

Now, as you close this book and put it away on a shelf, don't put your camera away as well. Get out, and *take some more photographs!* If you can't think of anything to take, you can always start again at Chapter 1!

Index

action photography, 49–56
animals, photographing, 19, 56–60. *See also Chapter 5*
apertures, 35, 38–9, 41–4, 62–4, 159–61
automatic cameras, 73–4, 158

'B' and 'T' settings, 102, 112, 122, 141
bellows, 167
black-out, 82–3
blank films and paper, 178
box cameras, 10, 79–80
bromide paper, 29–30, 81–4. *See also* printing paper *and* plastic-based paper
burning-in, 148–51

cable release, 103
camera shake, 39, 170–72
cameras, different types, 7–10, 65–80
cartridge-loading cameras, 7–8, 75–6, 166
cartridges, 128, 166
cassettes, 74, 128, 162
cathode head, 152–3
chemicals, 84–5, 125–7, 132, 134–5
chromogenic films, 135
close-up frame, 106–9

close-up lenses, 95–7, 102, 108–9
close-up photography, 20–21, 95–111. *See also Chapter 5*
coin test, 88
colour film, 27, 157, 164
colour processing, 27, 164
condensers, 152–4
contact printing, 30–32, 81–94, 138–9, 161
contact printing frame, 32
contrast grades (paper), 29, 83–4, 131, 154–5
contrast of negatives, 131, 174–5

dark-room for films, 124–5, 127–9
dark-room for printing, 81–94, 142
daylight printing, 24–33
dense negative, 175
depth of field, 46–8, 61–4, 98, 162–3
depth of focus, 64
developer, 85–6, 125, 131–5, 142
developing tanks, 133–4
developing times: films, 126, 133–4; paper, 89–90
'develop only', 24
diffuser, 152–4
dishes for processing, 86
dodging, 148–51
double exposure, 173

drying films, 130–31, 176
drying prints, 92–3

emulsion, 125, 127
enlarger lens, 141–2, 153
enlarger lighting, 152–4
enlargers, 137–40
enlarging, 136–55, 161–3
enprints, 24
exposure meter, 156–60
exposure settings, 35, 44, 115–17, 175

faults, 170–78
film speed ratings, 36, 45
films, types, 13, 135, 162, 164
filter factor, 165
filters, 164–5
fixer, 86–7, 127
flash, 117–23
flash synchronization, 113, 118
f numbers, 35, 38–9, 41–4, 62–4, 159–61
focal length, 43, 61, 163
focusing: camera, 37–9, 46–8, 61, 104–5, 172; enlarger, 144
focusing screen, 66, 104–5
focus magnifier, 144–5
fogging, 88, 124–5, 148, 154–5, 177
folding cameras, 8, 76–8

grain, 132, 144
ground glass, 103–4
guide numbers, 117–18

hardener, 127
houses, photographing, 14, 40. *See also Chapter 5*

incident light, 157–8
indoor photography, 21–2, 112–23. *See also Chapter 5*

infinity setting, 15
Instamatic cameras, 166
instant print cameras, 165–6

kink marks, 134, 176

lens cleaning, 167–8
lenses, enlarger, 141–2, 153
lenses, wide-angle and telephoto, 62, 163
light leak in camera, 167–9, 173
lines on film, 173, 176
loading a camera, 12–13

magnetic corners, 144
marks on films, 173–4, 176
marks on prints, 177–8
masking frame, 143–4
measure, making a, 87
mistakes, 170
models, photographing: *see* toys and models
monorail camera, 65–8
movements, 65–8

negatives, 25–8, 174–5

outdated film, 12
overexposure, 26

parallax, 101
people, photographing, 16–19, 48–56. *See also Chapter 5*
photoflood lights, 113
plastic-based paper, 30, 91, 93, 143, 162
Polaroid cameras, 165–6
printing paper, 28–30, 81–4, 142, 162. *See also* plastic-based paper
processing films, 124–35, 164
'process only', 24

reflected light, 157
roll film, 76, 128

safelight, 27, 82, 85–6, 88, 124
safety, 93, 143, 155
scratched negatives, 173, 176
second-hand cameras, 72, 76–7, 166–9
settings, 13, 34–6
shading, 148–51
shutter, 35, 166
shutter speeds, 35, 38–9, 41
single-lens reflex, 10, 68–71
specks on films, 174
speeds: *see* film speed ratings *and* shutter speeds
squeegee tongs, 130
stains, 87, 90, 177
stick for focusing, 108
stop bath, 87, 127

'T' and 'B' settings, 102, 112, 122, 141
temperature for processing, 90, 125
test strips, 90, 147
thirty-five mm cameras, 9, 73–5
time-and-temperature, 125
time exposures, 113–15
tongs, 91, 178
toys and models, photographing, 20, 99–100. *See also Chapter 5*
tripod, 98, 101
twin-lens reflex, 9, 71–3

underexposure, 26, 28, 175
unified system, 160–61

vibration, 161–2
viewfinders, 75, 99–100, 102
views, photographing, 16, 40. *See also Chapter 5*

washing films, 130
washing prints, 90–92
wetting agent, 130
white border, 144

zoom lens, 163